CHERRY AMES, ARMY NURSE

CHERRY AMES
ARMY NURSE

By

HELEN WELLS

SPRINGER **PUBLISHING COMPANY**

New York

Springer Publishing Company, Inc.
11 West 42nd Street, 15th Floor
New York, NY   10036-8002

Production Editor: Print Matters, Inc.
Cover design by Takeout Graphics, Inc.
Composition: Compset, Inc.

08 09 10/5 4 3

Library of Congress Cataloging-in-Publication Data

Wells, Helen, 1910–
  Cherry Ames, Army nurse / by Helen Wells.
    p. cm. — (Cherry Ames nurse stories)
  Summary: When she and her classmates in Spencer Hospital's
nurses training program enthusiastically sign up for the Army Nurse
Corps, Cherry Ames soon finds herself in Panama and struggling her
way through army regulations.
  ISBN 0-97715-972-8 (pbk.)
  [1. Nurses—Fiction. 2. Hospitals—Fiction. 3. World War,
1939–1945—Fiction. 4. United States. Army Nurse Corps—Fiction.
5. Panama—History—20th century—Fiction.] I. Title.

PZ7.W4644Cb 2005
[Fic]—dc22

2005051741

Printed in the United States of America

Contents

Foreword

Helen Wells, the author of the Cherry Ames stories, said, "I've always thought of nursing, and perhaps you have, too, as just about the most exciting, important, and rewarding, profession there is. Can you think of any other skill that is *always* needed by everybody, everywhere?"

I was and still am a fan of Cherry Ames. Her courageous dedication to her patients; her exciting escapades; her thirst for knowledge; her intelligent application of her nursing skills; and the respect she achieved as a registered nurse (RN) all made it clear to me that I was going to follow in her footsteps and become a nurse—nothing else would do. Thousands of other young people were motivated by Cherry Ames to become RNs as well. Cherry Ames motivated young people on into the 1970s, when the series ended. Readers who remember reading these books in the past will enjoy rereading them now—whether or not they chose nursing as a career—and perhaps sharing them with others.

My career has been a rich and satisfying one, during which I have delivered babies, saved lives, and cared for people in hospitals and in their homes. I have worked at the bedside and served as an administrator. I have published journals, written articles, taught students, consulted, and given expert testimony. Never once did I regret my decision to enter nursing.

During the time that I was publishing a nursing journal, I became acquainted with Robert Wells, brother of Helen Wells. In the course of conversation I learned that Ms. Wells had passed on and left the Cherry Ames copyright to Mr. Wells. Because there is a shortage of nurses here in the US today, I thought, "Why not bring Cherry back to motivate a whole new generation of young people? Why not ask Mr. Wells for the copyright to Cherry Ames?" Mr. Wells agreed, and the republished series is dedicated both to Helen Wells, the original author, and to her brother Robert Wells who transferred the rights to me. I am proud to ensure the continuation of Cherry Ames into the twenty-first century.

The final dedication is to you, both new and old readers of Cherry Ames: It is my dream that you enjoy Cherry's nursing skills as well as her escapades. I hope that young readers will feel motivated to choose nursing as your life's work. Remember, as Helen Wells herself said: there's no other skill that's *"always* needed by everybody, everywhere."

Harriet Schulman Forman, RN, Ed.D.
Series Editor

CHAPTER I

~~~~~~

On Her Way

"CHERRY! CHER-RY! COME QUICK! IT'S HERE!"

A sparkling, dark-haired girl suddenly popped out on the upstairs landing and hung over the staircase. Her cheeks were as red as her sweater and her black eyes shone with excitement. She took one look at her mother, gingerly holding up an envelope; another at her young friend Midge, hopping up and down with a strange lack of dignity for a fifteen-year-old.

"That's—*it!*" Midge cried. "Hurry up!"

Cherry swooped down the stairs and seized the official-looking envelope.

"What does it say?" Midge begged. Mrs. Ames, too, was trying to glimpse the letter over Cherry's shoulder.

"Here," Cherry said, absorbed, and allowed Midge to hold the empty envelope.

1

Midge read aloud the address in the left-hand corner with awe in her voice, "War Department, Official Business. Jiminy!"

"What does it say?" Mrs. Ames echoed Midge. She was a small, youthful, brown-eyed woman.

Cherry looked up and grinned. "This is what I've been waiting for every day of this two weeks' vacation! Harumph! You will please stand at attention while I read it to you." Cherry herself stood erect and read earnestly:

"By direction of the President, Cherry Ames is with her consent ordered to active duty with the Army of the United States, and assigned to the hospital unit as indicated. . . ." On graduating, Cherry had signed up with her whole nursing class to serve in the Army Nurse Corps. She already had indicated that she was available immediately and willing to serve overseas, and had sent in her photo, application, school record and State Board Examination record. Cherry took a deep breath and hurried on, ". . . and will proceed on 21 September this year to station specified for temporary duty pending activation Spencer Gen. unit."

There was another notice, too. "You are ordered to report to the Service Command at Wabash City . . . for Army physical examination!" . . . "Oh, gosh!" exclaimed Cherry.

"You have to weigh at least a hundred pounds and a lot of other things," Midge warned her.

"She'll pass," Mrs. Ames said, smiling at Cherry, "even the Army's rigid examination." Cherry's red cheeks and lips, her shining dark eyes, her eager, lively, pretty face, even her dancing black curls, fairly radiated vitality. She sparkled with youth and high spirits.

"Anyway," Cherry said with a great sigh, "I've already passed my two-day State Board Nurse examination. Now I can write R.N. after my name!"

Those proud letters, R.N., and the right to practice nursing, were privileges Cherry wanted with her whole heart. Just two weeks ago, she had completed her three years' nursing training at Spencer Hospital. Now she could hardly wait to put it into professional practice. Nursing was to be her personal gateway to adventure. With those two orders in her hand, Cherry knew she was going places—far and exciting places.

"No time to daydream," she said aloud, "I have to face an examination!"

"What," Midge asked practically, "is the date for that exam?"

"Oh, yes, dates. Time," Cherry said gloomily. Calendars and clocks were not her friends; she was always late. Her dark eyes fell on the dates in the letter and she jumped. "This letter must have been delayed! Or they don't believe in a fair warning! The Army physical is this afternoon! Oh!"

She tore out of the living room and up the stairs, calling back frantically, "Mrs. Ames, if you love your daughter, phone the station and find out when there's one of those jerky interurban cars! Midge, shine my best black shoes right away, and I'll treat you to as many banana splits as you can hold!" Her red sweater and flying black curls disappeared upstairs.

Mrs. Ames went to the phone and Midge raced off in pursuit of shoe blacking. Five minutes later, Cherry came tearing downstairs in her favorite red suit and beanie. She was panting and minus shoes, but every hair and button was in perfect order.

"Late but neat," she gasped. "When's my car?"

Her mother told her. Midge ran in with Cherry's shoes. Cherry wriggled into them, Midge consulted the clock, and Mrs. Ames laid out Cherry's fare. There was a round of good-bys and good wishes, and Cherry sprinted for the intercity streetcar.

She was halfway down the tree-lined block when her father's car pulled up to the curb beside her. He flung open the door.

"Hop in, Lieutenant. Where are you bound? I'll give you a lift."

"Lieutenant—if!" Cherry corrected her father as she jumped in. "It came, Dad . . . orders to report . . . I'm bound for Wabash City, for my Army physical. Gosh,

I'm glad you drove by this way! And where'd you get the gasoline in the midst of this shortage?"

"The war ration board heard I'm in the real estate business." Mr. Ames was a tall, good-humored looking man, with the blue eyes and fair hair which Charlie, brunette Cherry's twin, had inherited. "I'm driving out to a farm property," he said. "That's how you happen to be riding to your Army appointment in style."

"Ahem!"

Mr. Ames glanced at Cherry with a wry smile, as the car turned a corner. "Both my girl and my boy in the Army! The two Ames soldiers! And this Ames has to be an elderly stay-at-home."

"There's plenty to do on the home front to win," Cherry consoled him.

"Ye-es, but you and Charlie are going to be right in the thick of things!" Another minute, and her father drew up before the car stop to let Cherry out. "Good luck with the examination!" he called after her.

She grinned and clambered aboard the big trolley, not a minute too soon. Her father waved to her from the car, and then he was lost to view as the trolley bumped out of the north end of Hilton.

The Army Post nearest her home, to which Cherry was ordered to report, was the new post at Wabash City. Cherry settled herself in the dusty seat, noticing the numbers of young men in khaki uniform who filled the long car. They looked half-familiar to her, like her friends and schoolmates, like her own brother. Some of them looked lonesome, some tired, some were deep in their own thoughts. "Those are the boys I'm going to take care of," Cherry thought, and although many of them were older than herself, she felt motherly. It would seem funny to have only these lean, toughened, bronzed young men for patients. As a student nurse at Spencer Hospital, she had nursed everyone from children to old people. But Cherry recalled her nurse's pledge; to dedicate her life so that others might live . . . to help those who needed her, who without her help might die. "I guess the soldiers will need me most of all," she reflected soberly.

The half-hour ride from her own small town of Hilton to the Wabash City Army Post carried her through the wide, flat, Middle West prairie, with its enormous dome of blue sky. Now, in the first warm week of September, the acres of tall corn were still green, the cropped wheat fields still golden, and the farms with their fine red barns and great spreading trees enjoyed the last ripeness of summer. Watching from her car window, Cherry took a deep breath and calmed down. It was too late now to worry about this all-important examination, anyhow. But she had to pass it—she *had* to be an Army nurse!

Nursing always had been Cherry's dream. She knew it was the finest way a girl could serve people, and Cherry loved people and wanted to help them. Nursing was the way to put her idealism into practice.

Her inspiration had come from Midge's father, Dr. Joseph Fortune. The Ames's and the two lone Fortunes—for Midge's mother was dead—had been friends and neighbors in Hilton for years. Dr. Joe and Midge always had been an important part of Cherry's life. But recently, what a lot of changes the two families were experiencing! Dr. Fortune, and Cherry's twin brother Charles, and Cherry herself, were in Hilton very seldom these days. Dr. Fortune, to Cherry's great happiness, was doing research at her own Spencer Hospital. Charlie was a gunner in the Army Air Forces. And Cherry was going to be an Army nurse.

With both Charlie and Cherry away, Mr. and Mrs. Ames said their house seemed empty. Besides, Midge could not be left all alone. So Cherry's parents had closed up Dr. Fortune's cottage and taken Midge to live with them. Cherry looked down at Midge's shoe shine and grinned. The Ames family and the two Fortunes were, as Midge had said, "practically relatives by now, only nicer."

Cherry smiled again, thinking that she would be back at Spencer very soon. What happy times she had had there—and what exciting times! Even as a student nurse at Spencer, nursing had broadened her life and brought her new adventures, new understanding, new friends. "It won't be long now," she thought happily, "before I'll be seeing my pals, Ann and Gwen, and Lex, the darling, and 'my' Dr. Joe." They all were returning to the hospital to await the Army's call. Well, if she wanted to be a part of her country's vast Army, she had to pass this physical examination today. Cherry anxiously peered out of the trolley window. They were almost at Wabash City.

At Wabash City, Cherry found an open olive drab truck was going out to the post. Cherry climbed in. A dozen young soldiers smiled at her and made room for her on the uncomfortable wooden bench. The truck started down a rutted country road, and they all bounced together.

"You got a brother or a sweetheart out here?" asked a young man with a strong Western roll to his r's.

"No," said Cherry.

"Shucks, a young lady as pretty as that," said a boy with a Southern drawl. "Why, she's probably married to some lucky fellow on post."

"No," said Cherry, holding on tight to the side of the lurching truck and trying to look dignified.

"Going to work on the post?" a tall boy inquired.

"Going to tell the Old Man not to drill us so hard?" chuckled another one.

"Going to take pictures?" a redheaded boy asked eagerly.

"No," said Cherry. By this time she had to smile at their friendliness and at the assortment of accents from all over the country. "I'm going to be an Army nurse—I hope."

"Oh!" the young men all said, and Cherry was amazed to see a look of profound respect and warmth come into their faces. She was touched, too, and thoughtful, as the truck ground to a stop before a gate and some low, hastily constructed, wooden buildings.

"Well, I'd be happy to have you nurse me any old time," the Southern boy said, as he gallantly helped Cherry off the truck. "Now you want to go over to that little old building with the Red Cross flag, over yonder."

"She has to show her pass first," the tall boy interrupted.

Cherry pulled out the letter and showed it to the M.P.—the military policeman—at the gate. That young man—he could not have been much older than Midge, Cherry decided—looked at the letter. "You'll have to get a pass, Nurse, in that house over there."

Cherry looked about in bewilderment.

"We'll take her over!" volunteered three of the boys from the truck. Cherry found herself marched over with a military escort.

The whole afternoon was exciting. Cherry felt a glow of gratitude and an enormous liking for these swarms of friendly, hard-working young men in khaki, or in green fatigues, who crowded the dusty, sunny camp. Tanks

and jeeps roared by. Half a mile away, the sky was gray
with planes buzzing over the new airfield. Cherry decided
she was going to like Army life. Even the physical
examination, in which Cherry was tested from head to
toe by several specialists and all but turned inside out,
went off smoothly.

At the end of it, Cherry turned to the young nurse
who had been present throughout. "Do you think
I passed?" Cherry implored her.

"With those red cheeks?" The Army nurse laughed.
"Certainly you passed!"

Cherry's black eyes shone. "I've asked for overseas
duty—my whole class has!" she confided. She caught
herself wondering whether her young doctor friend Lex
had volunteered, too, for overseas duty.

"Well, good luck to you! And now," the post nurse told
her, "you'll follow Corporal Hart to the Administration
Building."

A very short corporal came in. He led Cherry briskly
across the post and into another wooden building. They
waited before one of the offices. Cherry saw long lines
of young men in civilian clothes, awaiting induction into
the Army. Everywhere there were young men, and more
young men.

Cherry looked at the columns of men for whose
health and lives she would be responsible. She stood up
a little straighter.

Then Cherry was in an office, being fingerprinted and saying yes, she was a citizen, yes, she could start at the drop of a hat, no, she had never been a policeman nor a fireman nor in jail. She was whisked off to see more and still more people. Then she was whirled away in another Army truck, and with her head now thoroughly spinning, she found herself back on a trolley.

She looked down at her nurse's wrist watch. Nearly six o'clock! But she was too preoccupied to pay any attention to the time. A new idea had popped into Cherry's head, and it troubled her. Did she really have the many stern qualifications required of an Army nurse?

Half an hour later, still thoughtful, she was home, answering her mother's and Midge's eager questions. She barely had taken her hat and coat off, when there was an uproar out on the porch.

"It's the Perkinses' dog after Mrs. Lane's cat again," Midge stated with satisfaction, as she tried on Cherry's red beanie. "Or vice versa."

Mrs. Ames cocked her head. "It sounds more like stamping and whistling to me," she said worriedly. "I do hope nobody is tearing up my flower beds."

Cherry listened too. The clamor was now increased by the steady ringing of the doorbell. Suddenly the truth struck her. There was only one person who could make all that noise—Charlie!

She raced to the door and there stood her twin brother—sunburned, silver wings on his chest, wide smile, and all. He and Cherry looked strikingly alike, even though he was taller and his keen eyes were sky-blue and his hair blond, while Cherry's eyes and hair were midnight dark.

"Anybody home?" he inquired calmly. "I was trying to give you folks a hint."

The Ames twins hugged each other, as Mrs. Ames and Midge came running. There was a profusion of hello's and how-are-you's and how-long-can-you-stay?

"Just a thirty-six-hour leave," Charlie told them. "I didn't want to waste a minute of it trying to phone you long distance that I was coming. I figured you'd let me in when I got here. How are you, Nurse? I beg your pardon—Lieutenant!"

"Whoa—I'm not safely in yet!" Cherry laughed.

"He—he just sort of dropped out of the sky!" Midge babbled. "Well, he always *was* crazy about planes!"

Mrs. Ames was talking excitedly into the phone. "Will? Will, Charlie's here! . . . Yes, just this moment . . . *Not* five minutes! Come on home right now!"

"When will you know if you're accepted?" Charlie asked Cherry.

"For heaven's sake, Cherry," Mrs. Ames protested, rushing up, "give the boy a chance to catch his breath!" Cherry shrugged helplessly, while Mrs. Ames asked him, "Are you hungry, dear? We'll have dinner right away! Do you want some clean laundry? Have you been all right?"

"Parents!" Charlie grinned sympathetically to Cherry.

That evening was given over to a joyous reunion. Cherry was too busy and too happy to worry over her new-found discovery—that being an Army nurse might involve more than a smart uniform and handsome soldiers and sailing away to exotic lands. Only when she went upstairs to pack, for she was leaving for Spencer Hospital the following morning, did she do some hard, realistic thinking.

Physical stamina, that was the first thing she or any nurse would need, and lots of it. Cherry decided she had that. Skilled nursing—thanks to her carefully chosen, really first-rate nursing school—was thoroughly trained into her. "I could nurse in my sleep," Cherry thought honestly. Courage. Character. We-ell, who could know that in advance? Cherry was inclined to plunge headlong into adventure and let courage take care of itself. It usually did. Maybe what she needed was less impulsiveness. What else? She would have to learn to strike just the right note with her soldier patients, not too familiar, and still with the warmth and understanding that was a big part of nursing. Military discipline? Cherry's heart hit bottom. Still, she was a nurse, and she was accustomed to hospital discipline. So far, so good.

But there was something else that worried her, some nameless self-doubt. Cherry sought to put it into words, as her hands folded garments and laid them in her new suitcase. But she could not name the worry that troubled her. All she knew was that she was thrilled and eager and scared.

Next morning, all those thoughts were pushed aside in the bittersweet hours before leaving home. Cherry was fairly tingling to be on her way, but good-bys were never easy. She wandered about the house, memorizing the pleasant comfortable rooms—the living room with its big fireplace and blue sofa and her grandmother's fragrant flower-petal jar, the dining room where a sunny bay window looked out on her mother's cherished flower garden. What parties they had had in these two big rooms! Every year, all the way through grammar school and high school, the Ames twins had invited all the neighborhood young people in to celebrate their joint birthday on the day before Christmas. Forty or fifty of them playing games and stuffing on birthday cake!

Cherry smiled and sighed and went upstairs. She peeked in at Charlie's plain, orderly room with the model airplanes he had built not so long ago. She stopped in at her parents' big cool room with the hand-patched rose quilt. It might be a long time before she saw these familiar things again.

At last Cherry went into her own gay little room and took a long last look around. Her window looked down on the lilac bush, which grew to her sill, and on the slender mulberry tree where the birds nested every year. She could hear them twittering now. She turned from the window and sat down a moment on the bed. It wore a cherry-red satin cover, with matching covers for her bed pillows, to make it a couch. The small bookshelves at its either end, against the white wall, the twin crystal lamps, the dressing table with its crisp white skirts, and the billowing white curtains tied with wide cherry-red ribbons—all these tempted her to stay. But Cherry could no more have stayed put, doing nothing, than she could have contentedly slept her life away. Her room would be waiting for her, in the exciting meantime.

And then her mother was calling to her that it was time to start, and Midge was rushing about bringing her the wrong gloves, and Charlie came upstairs for her suitcase. Her father had the car out in front; Cherry could hear the engine's impatient throbbing. She ran down the stairs, murmuring, "Good-by! Good-by! I'll come back to you some day!"

All through the streets of Hilton, Cherry was thinking that. First they drove through the quiet streets of pleasant homes, with children roller skating on the sidewalk, where Cherry had skated and sledded herself. The first early bonfires were burning pungently beside Victory gardens. They passed the big brick high school and, half-homesick, Cherry picked out "her" old windows as they drove by. They passed Dr. Joe's worn white cottage, closed up now, where Cherry had first seen the shining humane vision of medicine. Then downtown, through the busy well-kept streets with two- and three-story buildings, all kinds of shops, the four movie theaters, Cherry's favorite candy store, women she knew with bags of groceries in their arms, old Mr. Kyne's old horse still hitched to that grocery wagon. Cherry was finding it harder and harder to leave. She answered her family absently. It was a good thing she was being escorted to the station, for, left alone, her feet might have taken a route of their own right back to her home.

At the corner, Mr. Ames stopped the car for a traffic light. Cherry glanced idly at the corner window of a department store. What she saw made her sit up and catch her breath. It was a poster, and on it was a boy in khaki who looked like her own brother Charlie. His rifle was stuck upright into the earth; he was kneeling and clinging to the rifle with both hands, his head drooping.

Cherry's homesickness disappeared instantly. All the urgency she had felt before surged back now, redoubled. It was easy—it was imperative—to go now! Lose this war, and there would be no Hilton to come home to.

Cherry turned to find her mother's face drained of color.

"Mother!" Cherry said, and took her hand in her own. "Don't you get upset like that! They may get hurt, but they *can be saved*—the Army looks out for its men."

"He looks just like Charlie!" Then Mrs. Ames relaxed and leaned back against the seat. "You know, honey," she admitted, "I didn't want you to go. I didn't say so, but—I didn't. Now I guess I do. You're going to take my place, all the nurses are going to take the mothers' places, out there."

"That's the idea," Cherry reassured her. "And I'll write to you often." But now, she was impatient to be gone, on her way. She was glad that the train pulled in right away, and that there was little time for farewells.

It was what Charlie said that counted most. "I'll keep 'em flying and you'll put 'em back to flying. Good luck!" He saluted her.

"Good for you, Cherry," her father said soberly. He tucked a roll of bills into her purse, and bent and kissed her. "You're a brave girl."

Her mother clung to her. "God be with you, Cherry."

Midge was frankly letting the tears drip down her cheeks. "It's not that . . . I'm . . . worried about you," she got out between sobs. "But I can't . . . go too until I . . . stop flunking algebra!"

Cherry laughed and hastily hugged them all. "Don't worry—I'll write—take care of yourselves so *I* won't worry!" she said breathlessly. The engine let out a hoarse roar. A great pillar of white steam filled the air, and Cherry ran for the train. She hopped aboard and Charlie tossed her bag on after her, just as the wheels started to turn.

The last thing Cherry saw was her mother smiling and waving, and the wings on Charlie's broad chest shining very bright in the Middle West sun.

CHAPTER II

Lieutenant Ames Reporting

CHERRY WAS HAPPY. SHE WAS BACK AT SPENCER AND back on a hospital ward! Rows and rows of white beds were ranged along this long, white, still room, filled with quiet women patients. Two student nurses in blue and white scurried in and out of the ward kitchen and the ward's utility room. Beyond the ward windows, trees were turning gold and red in the vast yard, and the many white buildings of great Spencer Hospital stood like a fortress. Cherry walked down the row of beds, her crisp white uniform rustling, her pert nurse's cap perched on her black curls, thinking happily, "This is where I belong!"

She took a deep sniff of soap-and-medicines smell. It was a good satisfying feeling to be back at work again, even temporarily. Cherry was doing general floor duty

19

here on Women's Medical Ward for two weeks, until all her classmates came back and her Army unit was formed.

The ward phone tinkled. The head nurse, at her desk near the door, rose and answered it. "Ward 4, Mrs. Crane speaking. Yes, she's here," she said with some annoyance. She beckoned Cherry to come over, with a resigned frown on her middle-aged face. "Miss Ames, you're entirely too popular. This is the sixth call you've had on your very first day of duty! Can't your ex-classmates see you off duty?"

"But we haven't seen one another for all of two weeks!" Cherry teased. The head nurse smiled faintly but shook her head. "I'll tell them to stop it, Mrs. Crane," Cherry promised. "Hello!"

"That crone Crane!" said a lively girl's voice. "Well, it's only till we move in on Uncle Sam. Boy, I can hardly wait! Just got back to Spencer this minute—"

"Oh, yes, Miss Jones," Cherry said formally to Gwen. "I could see you around six. And would you please," she raised her voice for the head nurse's benefit, "advise the others that their continued telephone calls disturb ward routine?"

"All right, you Voice of Virtue," Gwen giggled knowingly. "See you at first dinner. Where's Ann?"

"I am unable to supply that information, Miss Jones," Cherry said professionally into the phone. "I suggest you apply at the office."

"I suggest you give the old dragon my love and kisses," Gwen laughed. "Good-by. Oh! Cherry! Bertha's waving a piece of paper in front of me and it says— wait—it says we're all to meet at seven-thirty to get our unit started!"

"Already? Hold on! What else does it say?" Cherry asked quickly. But Gwen had hung up. Cherry reluctantly hung up, too.

"Not a personal call?" Mrs. Crane said, softening.

"Uh . . . an inquiry and a notice," Cherry gulped, and became extremely busy giving the patients their afternoon care. A most important notice! Things were rolling even faster than she had expected.

A little before six, Cherry raced over to Spencer Hall, the hospital's main building, and into the nurses' attractive pale green dining room. She hurriedly filled her tray at the food counter and then peered into the crowds at the tables, looking for Gwen's red head. The big room was jammed with graduate nurses in all-white, with student nurses in striped blue-and-white dresses, white aprons and caps, and with shy and humble beginners in probationer's gray, sans bib and sans cap.

Cherry wiggled herself and her tray through the tables, exchanging hello's with cool blond Marie Swift and Vivian Warren. She greeted Josie Franklin, whose eyes behind their glasses looked like a frightened rabbit's. Bertha Larsen waved hello to her too. Finally she reached Gwen.

"Here's Ames!" Gwen's merry freckled face crinkled up in a smile.

Quiet little Mai Lee was with her. The Chinese girl pulled out a chair for Cherry, and Cherry sat down. She grew excited when she saw how excited all her old classmates were.

"What's the news? Will someone kindly tell me?"

"I don't know where to start!" Gwen exclaimed. "They're going to send someone over from the Army in a few days—maybe it'll be a romantic officer! And we're going to be what's called an affiliated unit. We nurses, and our own Spencer doctors and technicians, will all stay together because we're already used to working together."

"How many of us?" Cherry asked breathlessly.

Mai Lee looked amused but she replied, "Well, there were sixty in our class, so that's sixty nurses. Then there will be at least three doctors. The names were posted just ten minutes ago. Dr. Hal Freeman and that nice Dr. 'Ding' Jackson and *your* Dr. Lex Upham, Cherry." Cherry's heart rose at this news, but she was not surprised. "Anaesthetists and X-ray and laboratory people, of course. *And*—" Both Mai Lee and Gwen groaned.

"What's the matter?" Cherry asked in alarm. "Have you both a stomach-ache?"

Gwen stuck her flaming head forward. "Watch your own stomach sink! Guess who's going to be our unit's chief surgeon and unit director!"

Cherry guessed and shrank in her chair. "Don't say it's Dr. Wylie," she pleaded.

"Yes, my love, the very same." Gwen took a drink of water as if to revive herself. Dr. Wylie was senior surgeon of Spencer, one of the Administrators of Spencer, and nationally famous. He would—Cherry knew from previous experience—direct them within an inch of their young lives. Gwen explained that Dr. Wylie, who had been working for six months at the battle fronts, felt he now was more urgently needed to form and direct a new unit.

"I'm nearly as frightened of your Dr. Marius Lexington Upham as I am of Dr. Wylie," Mai Lee admitted.

Gwen nodded ruefully. "He's just too brilliant to be human!"

"He's perfectly human!" Cherry defended him. "You idiots just never got to know him because you're scared of him, and you're scared of him because you don't know him—if you follow me."

"Follow a tornado like Lex?" Gwen said. "Not Gwen Jones! If Cherry can handle him, it's at her own risk! By the way, is Dr. Joe Fortune coming with our unit?"

But the girls did not know, not even Cherry.

"What's worrying me," Josie Franklin blurted out from the next table, "is those corpsmen. I don't want to be in charge of any soldiers and give orders and train them, even if they are going to help us nurse and everything. What am I going to do with six soldiers?" she wailed. "Do I look like a military woman?"

Cherry burst out laughing. "Never mind," she consoled Josie. "We're going to take a lot of orders before we start giving any!"

They rose and strolled out to the huge rotunda. Cherry looked around at the library, the reception room, even the offices, and pictured the white wards and operating rooms upstairs. "I really love this hospital," she thought. "It's my second home. Now see here, Ames, you aren't going to get homesick a second time, are you?"

Gwen beside her was looking around, too, and frowning. "Lots of familiar faces gone, aren't there?"

It was true: the younger doctors and nurses were streaming out of Spencer to join the Army and Navy. But there were many new student nurses and internes stepping in to man the hospital, faces Cherry had never seen before. She was relieved to see these new young people.

Just then a young man strode into the rotunda from the yard. He was solidly, even massively, built, with an alert, intelligent face. His eyes and decided brows were much darker than his straight sandy hair. His lordly stride, his impatient commanding manner, proclaimed him someone out of the ordinary.

"Lex!" Cherry whirled around and smiled at him warmly.

His returning smile lighted up his young, aggressive face. He caught up with her and Gwen. "Hi, Cherry! You're looking wonderful! Have a good vacation?" he asked Gwen genially, and turned to say a friendly hello to Mai Lee and Bertha and Marie Swift and the others. The nurses smiled back, but they were too respectful to be at ease. It was rumored that even Dr. Wylie once had stood corrected by the brilliant and unpredictable Dr. Lex Upham.

"Tornado!" Cherry saw Gwen's lips form the word. One by one, and not as inconspicuously as they thought, the girls fled into the big sitting room. Cherry hoped Lex would not notice, but he stood looking after them like a child who is left out of a party. Then he turned back to Cherry and beamed at her.

"I missed you," he said.

"In these two little weeks?" Cherry laughed. "Didn't you take a vacation? Everyone else did."

"Well . . . I . . . you see . . . I got to experimenting with some new hormones, helping Dr. Fortune, and it was so interesting I couldn't tear myself away. It's like playing detective with a microscope."

"So you forgot me for a hormone! Fine loyal friend you are!" Cherry scoffed.

"If you're jealous of a hormone, you ought to meet my fascinating new bacillus. I've named it for you."

"So now I look like a bug to you," Cherry said with a straight face. "And don't tell me I am deliberately misunderstanding you!"

Lex's face darkened like a thundercloud. His temper exploded so quickly—and his sense of humor popped up again so promptly—that Cherry, who was quick-tempered herself, never could resist teasing him. He caught the laughter in her eyes.

"This time I don't bite," he told her. "See here, Cherry. Do I have to go into that sitting room for the meeting with all those girls?"

"I'll protect you, Lex," said a cool, feminine voice. A quiet, brown-haired girl had come up. She was wearing a dark blue suit that matched her steady eyes, and she was carrying a suitcase.

"Ann Evans!" Cherry cried, as Lex relieved her of her suitcase. "I looked for you on the Wabash train—I thought you'd get on about an hour after I did. And here you show up a whole day late!"

"I was sick. But I notified Miss Reamer," Ann replied. "Have I missed anything important?"

"The meeting for Spencer unit is just starting," Lex said. "Come on, ladies."

The sixty nurses from Cherry's class filled the big sitting room. Lex found Dr. "Ding" Jackson and Dr. Freeman there, and the three young men laughingly huddled together—"for masculine security," lanky "Ding" said.

The meeting was largely routine, the first but exciting steps toward getting themselves organized. Cherry looked about at the familiar faces and wondered in what far lands they would some day find themselves. She wondered, too, whether Dr. Joe was coming with them. Leaning over to where Lex sat, she whispered a question to him. Lex should know: he assisted Dr. Joe in his research.

He wrote back a note, in his firm small script. "Don't know exactly. Very secretive. Something about his malaria serum experiment." While Cherry was reading it, he reached for the note and added, "We'll miss him if he doesn't."

Cherry went to see Dr. Joe the following afternoon when she went off ward duty. She found him in his laboratory in Lincoln Hall. As usual, it was littered with notes, basins, test tubes, and half-empty tins of tobacco. Dr. Joe himself, in a rumpled white lab coat, his thick short gray hair rumpled too, was leaning dreamily against the wall, sucking on a cold pipe. Cherry recognized the usual signs; he was thinking something out. She kept silent, affectionately watching him.

Cherry was very fond of Midge's father, gentle, studious, impractical Dr. Joseph Fortune. Dr. Joe had helped Cherry and her twin brother Charlie into the world, and Dr. Joe had been her inspiring friend ever since. When Mrs. Fortune died, Cherry—though she was still in high school—had kept an eye on madcap Midge and on absent-minded Dr. Joe. She had helped him with his medical research in his little kitchen laboratory, she had encouraged him when no one else believed in his research. It was Dr. Joe's devoted example that had sent Cherry to Spencer Nursing School. And it was Cherry's efforts that finally helped Dr. Joe to win his present recognition. She wondered, watching him now, why he was so mysterious about his immediate plans. Finally she said aloud, jokingly:

"Is anyone here?"

Dr. Joe smiled and turned to her. "Hello, my dear. How is Hilton and everyone? How is Midge? I hope your mother isn't worn out with her."

"Midge is in top form, and everyone is fine." Cherry scanned his tired though still boyish face. "Are you all right, Dr. Joe?"

"I'm a little worried," Dr. Joe admitted. But he made no move to say what he was worried about. Cherry, of course, did not ask questions. "I had a letter from Midge just this morning," Dr. Fortune continued. "It seems she—By the way, child, have you seen Dr. Wylie?"

"*I* see Dr. Wylie? Heavens, no!"

"Hmm. Must talk to him about getting his authorization for my further research. He doesn't like what I want to do—and where I want to try it out."

Cherry tried to look polite, interested, encouraging and not inquisitive. But Dr. Joe merely wandered about the laboratory, absently picking things up and setting them down again. Then he remembered that she was there, and smiled at her. His thoughtful eyes studied her.

"Are you excited about going into the Army Nurse Corps?"

Cherry threw back her black curls and laughed. "Thrilled—and chilled!" Dr. Joe looked puzzled. "A little frightened," she explained.

"Of what?"

As usual with Dr. Joe, Cherry had to think about essentials. "I'm not frightened of bullets or maybe going hungry or . . . or any physical danger. I'm frightened about something that's in myself—or perhaps isn't in me."

Dr. Joe nodded. "You are putting yourself to the great test. It's a healthy sign that you're frightened—you realize the seriousness of what you are facing. It won' t be easy. It will call on every resource you possess, and perhaps more maturity than you have at present."

Cherry listened humbly. "But a nurse is a soldier, even

in peacetime. And you always were a determined little monkey." He patted her glowing cheek.

Cherry grinned. "If you mean I can't and won't stay put, yes! Monkeys are pretty restless and inquisitive creatures, you know."

The rest of that week, Cherry felt restless indeed. Now that the unit was really forming, she could hardly wait to launch on the great adventure. She competently raced through her daily work on the ward, and then fretted until time to go off, when she scampered about the hospital for news. September fifteenth was a great day. Cherry received another of those official-looking envelopes. The Army was pleased to notify her that she had passed her first physical examination. Cherry virtually danced about the ward that day.

Some more excitement was going on at Spencer. New student nurses were pouring in, and some of the older students were returning from their month's vacation. Cherry noticed, in growing numbers, a certain stunning red-trimmed gray uniform, worn with a dashing gray beret. Most of the new girls sported it. Cherry half envied them. She knew what it was: the U.S. Cadet Nurse Corps. Those lucky girls were getting their nursing training free, with their rooms at Spencer and their meals and uniforms and pocket money provided for them, too. When there was a knock on Cherry's door in the senior-and-graduate Residence Hall Monday evening, Cherry was not surprised to see Mildred Burnham, her "probie adoptee." But when Mildred smiled back at her from under a gray beret and drew forward another young girl in jaunty gray, Cherry frankly whistled.

"How'd you get it? And who's this?" she demanded, as the two girls came into her gay little chintz-and-maple room. "Sit down and tell me all!" She brought out a box of candy, half-full, and the girls settled themselves.

Mildred smiled confidently. Cherry had never seen her head held so high. "I received it by applying and qualifying. I'm a junior now, you know, Cherry, but I was able to transfer to the Cadets in midstream. And this is my cousin, Nurse Cadet Louise Woods. She's a probie—she's just started her training."

Louise was a small pretty girl who could not have been a minute over seventeen. She smiled shyly at Cherry, awed by a graduate nurse.

"We finish our training in two and a half years instead of three," Mildred announced, "and then we can spend the last six months in Army or Navy hospitals, or public health nursing, or civilian hospitals, depending on what we want to do." She told Cherry that, because of the shortage of nurses, she already had offers of positions even before graduation.

Louise said shyly, "Everyone warned me nursing was *awful*. But you know nursing is *fun!* Even with all the terrific mistakes I make! Why, I never had such a good time in my life!"

Cherry and Mildred laughed, remembering their own probie days. "I know," Cherry said sympathetically, "I discovered that too."

While the two older girls discussed their careers, Louise concentrated on Cherry's chocolates.

When they were leaving, Louise—who was obviously proud of her smart gray uniform—asked Cherry if a Cadet were required to salute a Lieutenant.

"No, but you can if you want to!" Cherry laughed. "But as a matter of fact, I ought to salute you for the work you are doing."

"My work?" said the astonished probationer. Mildred, too, looked puzzled. "I wish I were going to save soldiers' lives like you. But no, I have to stick around here doing little jobs, like folding bandages and taking temperatures and making the patients swallow their medicine."

"Little things!" Cherry shook her head. "Those are big things. And you *are* helping to save soldiers' and sailors' lives! For every new girl who starts her nursing training, a graduate nurse can be released to the Army. If you and

Mildred weren't on the job here, I'd have to stay and do your work."

Cherry saluted little Louise, who visibly expanded with pride. She called good night to Mildred, and watched their trim gray figures disappear down the hall. Louise was cute, even if she had eaten up all her chocolates.

The next morning, on her way to breakfast, Cherry found another of those official envelopes waiting for her. Cherry Ames, R.N., Spencer Hospital, was ordered to report in person to the Commanding Officer at Fort Herold, New Jersey, for duty, on September twenty-first. This was the nineteenth! Cherry raced through the rest of the form letter. Her serial number was given, the letter N and a long string of numbers. She'd have to memorize that. It was her identification and the key to her Army records. There were orders about her equipment, pay, expenses, travel allowances. Cherry read the orders but she was so excited, the information did not register. She could only think dazedly, "We're actually starting!" She hurried off to find the other girls. They all were in the nurses' dining room, in a state between joy and panic. Josie Franklin was taking her own temperature. No one ate any breakfast, but cups and cups of black coffee were consumed.

Later that morning ward phones rang all over the hospital; nurses going with the Spencer unit were summoned off the wards, their Spencer duty was permanently canceled, and they were directed to go to the auditorium directly after noon dinner. Cherry bolted a sandwich with the others and hurried to the auditorium. She was startled to find a soldier at the door, checking off their names and admitting them one by one.

A murmur of crackling white uniforms and subdued voices filled the room. They did not have long to wait. Dr. Wylie, stern, gray-haired, stocky, and in uniform, and Miss Reamer, the gracious Superintendent of Nurses, came in with two Army officers. The four people mounted the empty stage.

Dr. Wylie, now Lieutenant-Colonel Wylie, stomped forward to the speaker's stand. "I wish to salute you young women who are about to become Army nurses! You will take the first steps today. And we leave for Fort Herold tomorrow afternoon." From there on, Colonel Wylie glowered and scolded, as if doubting that they had the minds of gnats. But he gave them every bit of information they needed.

The two Army officers were introduced and each spoke briefly. Major Roberts, a middle-aged doctor from the Medical Corps, instructed them on the immediate steps of entering the Army Nurse Corps. Their chief nurse—the Army equivalent of head nurse—would be assigned to them at Post. Captain Endicott, a young man, was not a doctor but an officer from the regular Army. He instructed them about transportation, orders, pay and allowances. Both officers were terse, clear, quick, concerned for the best welfare of these soldiers-to-be.

Then Miss Reamer rose. She was almost as thrilled as the girls themselves. "Will you form a single line and come up here on the platform, one by one?"

They lined up, Cherry between Gwen and Ann. Major Roberts and Lieutenant-Colonel Wylie were talking earnestly together. Captain Endicott sat at a table with the girls' records, and talked briefly to each nurse as she came up. Cherry noticed Lex enter the auditorium, mount the stage, and speak to Dr. Wylie.

Captain Endicott was, Cherry saw at closer view, a strikingly handsome and sleek young officer. He had regular features, clear gray eyes, wavy blond hair, and fine, well-kept hands. He undeniably had charm, and he knew it.

"Your name, please?" he asked.

"Cherry Ames."

He pulled out her cards and asked, "Are you prepared to travel very soon?"

"Yes, sir, I'm ready to go anywhere in the world! I've even," she added humorously, "bought seasick remedy."

Captain Endicott looked at her quizzically. "Will you need seasick remedy in New Jersey?"

"New Jersey?" Cherry scoffed. "That's only the jumping-off spot to a long boat ride."

"The long boat ride," Captain Endicott chuckled, "comes *after* you complete your training. I merely meant to ask, are you ready to travel immediately?"

"Yes, sir, I'm prepared to be off at the drop of a military hat," Cherry twinkled back at him.

Cherry finished answering the rest of Captain Endicott's questions. She started to turn away, when the handsome Captain called to her:

"Oh, Miss Ames. Don't forget your water wings!"

"No, sir, nor my paddle," was the swift repartee. They both burst out laughing. As she walked away, still smiling, she was suddenly aware that Lex was taking in the whole interview, his dark brows knitted in a frown.

Cherry finished and went down the platform steps. There was Lex waiting for her. Still frowning, he drew her to one side.

"You seem to find the handsome captain amusing!" Lex said in that brusque way of his.

"Don't be silly, Lex," Cherry said, with some irritation. She knew by now that she should not let Lex's impulsive, highhanded manner arouse her own quick temper. But somehow it always did.

Lex said trenchantly, "Do you suppose anything else about him measures up to his looks?"

Cherry took another quick look at Endicott. He was smiling, almost preening. Instantly she saw what Lex meant. Lex, who had lightning insight into character, who despised sham, was absolutely right.

"He seems to turn on the charm for all the girls," Cherry agreed. "But you don't have to be so snappish about it."

"Just look at him," Lex retorted. Cherry saw Captain Endicott, very businesslike of course, smile his nicest at Ann Evans. Ann remained unimpressed.

Vivian Warren went up to his table next. Cherry watched her with particular affection and a feeling of protectiveness. Three years ago, when all the girls were just entering nurses' training, Vivian had been a cold, embittered girl, without friends. But Cherry had discovered that Vivian, behind her defiant front, was hiding a life of poverty and unhappiness, and was really frightened and starved for affection. Now the coldness, the harsh make-up, the fear, were gone. It was Cherry who had helped Vivian blossom out into the sweet-faced girl who stood now, slight and rather nervous, before Captain Endicott's table. There was something a little wistful, a little pathetic, in Vivian's pretty face.

Captain Endicott spoke to Vivian as he went through her cards. Cherry could not hear what they were saying. But she saw Vivian smile and stand up a little straighter, eager to please and to be liked. And Captain

Endicott promptly noticed Vivian's unusual responsive-
ness. He made his smile even brighter.

Cherry turned to Lex. "There, you see! You needn't
warn me. I'd better warn Vivian!"

Cherry could understand that Vivian might be dazzled
by this suave young captain. And Cherry suspected that
Captain Endicott, with his obvious vanity, would
encourage Vivian's admiration.

Vivian finished and came over to Cherry and Lex. Her
soft hazel eyes were glowing, a faint pink flushed the
fine, pale skin of her sensitive face. "Isn't Captain
Endicott nice!" she exclaimed.

Lex snorted and abruptly walked away.

"I think Captain Endicott is awfully nice looking and
pleasant-mannered," Cherry said carefully.

Vivian caught the doubt in her voice at once. She
looked at Cherry disappointedly. "You mean perhaps
he isn't as nice as I think?"

"It's just," Cherry said in a light tone, "that going away
with the unit is more thrilling just now than any young
man! Don't you feel that way?"

Vivian said softly, "He's going to be at our camp, too,
you know."

Cherry laughed. "Here, here, keep your pretty head!
There are going to be lots of nice young men at camp,
Vivian. Perhaps some even nicer than this one. Why

don't you reserve judgment—and anyhow, we have to pack."

Vivian smiled and went out of the auditorium with Cherry.

The rest of that day, the nurses hastily packed and hurried through last-minute errands and shopping. Cherry was so excited that everything seemed faintly unreal to her. The Superintendent of Nurses had asked them to be in the big lounge at three. With their bags bulging and strapped, they all went over to Spencer Hall for what they supposed was one more official meeting. But at the threshold they were surprised to find the long table before the fireplace laid for tea, brilliant autumn leaves everywhere, and Miss Reamer entertaining a distinguished-looking man. Miss Reamer was sending them off in style with a farewell reception!

The visitor had come from the Red Cross to honor Cherry's class for signing up unanimously in the Army Nurse Corps. After a brief speech, he presented them with a citation.

Just as the speaker finished, Cherry saw Dr. Joe softly come in. He was wearing the uniform of an Army Major and looked very happy. He beckoned to Cherry. Under cover of the applause, she slipped over to him.

"I'm going with your unit after all!" Dr. Joe told her in a whisper.

Cherry was so delighted she could have hugged him then and there. "What—and where—?" she started.

"I'll have to tell you some other time," Dr. Joe promised. He moved off to meet other staff doctors who were coming in to celebrate Spencer's first unit.

On the surface, the party was gay, with everyone talking and circulating and laughing a great deal. But Cherry caught a glimpse of Miss Reamer's face, off guard: it was sober and deeply moved. Cherry realized that was how they all were really feeling. Here was a little band of them, going out to spread Spencer's long tradition of service and devotion. Every doctor and nurse in this room loved Spencer Hospital, and everyone's heart went with this unit, venturing out into war in Spencer's name.

Miss Reamer spoke to them. "There isn't much I can say," she began. "I have known every one of you young women since you came here as probationers, and I've known you well all through your student years. Now, to see you set forth is like seeing my own daughters go." She smiled at them, one by one, a little shakily. Her eyes met Cherry's, and Cherry felt very tangibly the love this older teacher and guide had for them all. "But I'm nearly forgetting your gift!" Miss Reamer turned for a moment to get something from the table. "Spencer School of Nursing presents this flag to Spencer Hospital. It will hang in the rotunda, in your honor, as long as this hospital stands!"

She unfurled a great gleaming white service flag, bordered in dark blue. The school's name and the year of Cherry's class were sewn on it. A murmur of delight went up from the young nurses. Cherry swallowed a lump in her throat. Instead of sixty stars, for the sixty girls in service, the flag bore sixty miniature nurse's caps!

~~~~~~

CHAPTER III

Lovey

FORT HEROLD STRETCHED OUT FOR MILES, AN ORDERLY blueprint in the low, wandering, eastern hills. The warm afternoon sun beat down on its miles of white-painted buildings. Cherry bounced along on the bus, with Gwen falling in her lap, and hung out the open window to see three other busses full of Spencer nurses roaring along behind. They had boarded the train yesterday right after Miss Reamer's tea, and now they were finally here.

Down the road they thundered. The blueprint grew bigger and nearer. Cherry could see khaki figures moving, and a far-off burst of gunfire, followed by lingering smoke.

"This is it!" called Captain Endicott from the front of her bus. They swerved into the gate, halted momentarily for the guard, then drove slowly and smoothly into camp. Cherry stared. She had never seen a place so beautiful!

Fort Herold, long-established and one of the Army's proudest posts, looked like a beautiful green park when you first rode down its curving, tree-lined drives. Here stood simple, stately, red-brick, white-pillared Administration buildings, in typical American style. Their bus followed the road along the long parade ground, richly bordered on either side by trees and by red-brick homes with beautifully kept lawns. Officers' Row, Captain Endicott explained. Far away, facing the end of the parade ground, and heading Officers' Row, was the Colonel's house, surrounded by gardens. Captain Endicott identified the buildings which dotted the paved walks and the green sweep of park: Officers' Club, the Guest House for soldiers' visitors, the restaurant, the gay-looking cafeteria, the Post Exchange store. Cherry looked and looked.

What surprised Cherry, however, was that there were so few people about. She had expected a great bustle of soldiers and jeeps and tanks. But only single soldiers walked briskly on any of the paths, exchanging salutes with officers as they passed, only a few cars and jeeps drove quietly by; some children played before Officers' Row.

"Where is everybody?" she asked.

Captain Endicott smiled his winning smile. "Do you see those woods way off to the northeast end of Post?" They all stared, first over the low roofs of miles of long, one-story, white-painted, wooden barracks, then to the woods. "Some of the men are out there, doing radio work. Some of the others—listen!" Cherry waited, then heard a faint rattle of gunfire. The sunny air moved in waves. "They're shooting on the rifle range—that's a good safe distance away. Now look over there," he said, as the bus swerved. "Look hard."

Cherry scowled toward the distant road. She saw nothing but trees and blowing autumn leaves. Captain Endicott grinned. She stared again, watching as hard as she could. The whole road seemed to be moving!

"Have I gone crazy?" Vivian demanded, seeing it too.

The young captain laughed as if Vivian had said something particularly delightful. "That's a company going out on maneuvers for the night. They're wearing field camouflage suits, that's why you have a hard time seeing them. There are a hundred and eighty men moving along that road." He signaled two soldiers at the back of the bus to collect the girls' luggage, and added casually, "There are forty thousand men training on this Post."

"Are they going to walk far?" Josie Franklin inquired, with one fascinated eye on the deceptive road, the other anxiously on her suitcase.

"They'll march about twenty miles today. Oh, don't look so scared!" Captain Endicott teased the girls as their faces changed. "You'll be taking sizable hikes yourselves, and wearing camouflage and flinging yourselves in foxholes in a day or two."

"We will?" Cherry gulped. All the other girls were listening, wide-eyed. They did not notice that the bus was slowing down.

"Certainly. You're going to have basic training like any soldier, except for handling guns. Don't you want to know how to protect yourselves in case there's no military man around to protect you?" He smiled at Cherry engagingly—just the sort of smile that she did not care for, Cherry thought.

"We-ell, yes, but," said Cherry, and she spoke for all of them, "what about nursing? I don't even see the hospital buildings."

"Right here." Captain Endicott's handsome face looked amused. "All out, please!"

Cherry clambered down. She found herself in a deserted, unpaved street, lined with rows and rows of long, one-story, wooden hospital buildings, which looked like barracks—"or shoe boxes," thought Cherry. The hospital buildings were in a quiet area at the edge of the Post. "Surgical," said a sign on one building. "Medical W-l," another sign said. On the screened-in porch of W-l, two boys in maroon bathrobes were sitting limply in rocking chairs. At the end of the street stood the big brick Main Hospital with an American flag, and under it, a Red Cross flag.

"Now you'll meet the Chief Nurse," Captain Endicott said. With official papers in hand, and last-minute tugs at their hats, the girls trooped after him into the Main Hospital. "It looks like any other hospital," Cherry thought, half-disappointed but reassured. Captain Endicott ushered them into a big office. He had suddenly become stiff and formal.

"This is Lieutenant Glenn," he said, as a young nurse smilingly rose from her desk. "She is the Chief Nurse's assistant." He managed an extra, pointed glance at Vivian before he left. Cherry was annoyed. She might have been less annoyed had she known that this would be the last they would see of Captain Endicott for the next two wild weeks.

The Chief Nurse came in. She was a rather grim-looking individual, a large square woman with clipped gray hair. Cherry noticed the gold caduceus with the letter N of the Medical Corps on the left side of her white uniform collar, and the silver ash leaf of Lieutenant-Colonel on the right side, as she listened to her somewhat chilling greeting. It appeared that they would have to get into the swing of things immediately, there was no time to lose. However, from now until suppertime, they might walk about camp "to adjust themselves." She warned them that once Sergeant Deake took over, they would have little freedom. Cherry suspected she probably would not see this stern Chief Nurse often, and she was not sorry.

"But who is Sergeant Deake?" Ann wanted to know. They had escaped outdoors again, after filling out a number of forms.

"Sergeant Deake will reveal himself soon enough," Cherry predicted. "Let's all go sight-seeing while we can."

So for the rest of the afternoon, Cherry with her friends trotted, then trudged, then limped, all over Fort Herold. They saw pretty little chapels, three trim white movie houses, recreation halls, mess halls, libraries, repair shops, the enormous motor pool, the high water tower which Cherry used as a landmark against getting lost, the fire department, jeeps all over the place, men drilling and exercising and wrestling and marching, miles and miles and more miles of neat barracks. "This is a complete world!" Cherry declared. "Only— oh, my feet!"

It was a relief to go at last to Nurses' Quarters. It was one of those beautiful brick buildings with long verandas. Each girl had her own attractive room, sharing the bath with the girl next door. Their luggage was awaiting them. Pleasant Lieutenant Glenn, the Chief Nurse's assistant, showed them the handsome sitting room and library downstairs, and added, "I'm your house mother, in addition to my other duties."

"No dining room?" Bertha Larsen asked hungrily.

Lieutenant Glenn laughed. "If you want supper, you'll have to hike to Nurses' Mess."

Hike they most certainly did. Cherry thought they would never get there. Vivian groaned that it must be at least ten miles.

"I just hope," Cherry said grimly, "that supper is worth it."

A good hearty supper, served in a big hall, cheered her, and the presence of friendly older nurses was cheering, too. But then, Cherry realized, she would have to walk all the way back again!

"We'll take it in easy stages," Cherry decided, as they all started out across the shadowy Post. Lighted windows gleamed here and there, and khaki-clad figures drifted by. Cherry wished she would bump into Lex. They passed rows of barracks, each with its brooms and mops hanging neatly out in front, the men sitting on the front steps, smoking and talking. Staggering on, they dropped onto soda fountain stools at the crowded cafeteria, and strengthened themselves with cokes and swing records on the juke box. "I could sleep on a plank tonight!" Cherry declared. "On a piano! On a washboard! On *anything!* I'm adjusted, but my feet aren't!"

By ten o'clock the Post was darkened and growing quiet. Cherry fell into bed, already in love with this orderly, comradely Army world. It was her world now. She belonged!

She awoke next morning to the brassy call of bugles. Cherry got into her own white nurse's uniform and cap and her old navy blue cape, double-quick time. Dawn breakfast—then the Chief Nurse swore them into office, for the duration of the war plus six months. There would be no backing out now! They met Colonel Dorsey, the Post's Commanding Officer. Then they were whisked through another physical examination, and given inoculations. Next, they tried on uniforms— all white for ward duty, with an olive drab cape to wear on Post. This was the uniform Cherry would wear here at Herold, starting this morning. For outdoors and dress wear, they were fitted for an officer's handsome suit and cap, all superb tailoring and gold Army insignia. Fine russet leather gloves and matching bag completed the uniform. For field work, they received a dust-colored coverall. Red Cross arm bands came next. Then Cherry tried on her dashing olive drab trench coat, with a button-in lamb's-wool lining. Off they rushed again— this time to the lecture hall.

Just as Cherry was going into the hall, a young lieutenant was coming out. He politely stood aside and saluted. She gulped with surprise and hastily managed to salute back. At the foot of the stairs, two over-conscientious privates saluted her as they passed. Cherry jumped again, but she painfully saluted. "I now am," she reminded herself, remembering her oath of office, "by Act of Congress, an officer and a lady. And I certainly am being treated as such!"

The rest of the girls, as they sank rather bewildered into the lecture hall chairs, were fumblingly trying to practice the salute. Their amused lecturer taught them to salute, first of all.

Cherry liked all five instructors—the three older Army nurses and the two male Administrative officers. In rapid succession, they told her she was part of the Army now, would go anywhere and stay as long as needed, and share the Army's responsibility to supply medical and nursing care for its sick and wounded men. "Nurses are the first women to reach the front lines," the eldest Army nurse told them proudly, "and often the only women." That was all right with Cherry! She learned that the Army had all kinds of hospitals—large general hospitals with a thousand to two thousand beds; station hospitals, equally big or for only a hundred and fifty men; small post hospitals like Herold's. In combat zones, the Army might ask Cherry to work in a surgical hospital or an evacuation unit or a field hospital. She might ride a hospital ship or train or plane. Sometimes nurses and doctors formed shock teams and went right into the smoky deafening air of battle.

"The need for nurses is so urgent," the lecturer continued, "we must ship you out soon, so you will have your four weeks' basic training immediately." It turned out that right through all four weeks they would be entrusted to Sergeant Deake's mercies for drill and calisthenics. For the last two weeks, they would nurse under supervision on the Post's wards. Finally, they would go out with the troops on maneuvers. Just then, bugles and drums struck up a thundering march from the practice room near by, and the lecturer hoarsely shouted the rest.

Right now, for the first two weeks, they would have classes in ward management and nursing practice (Army style), including all the reports and paper work, transportation and care of the wounded, military discipline, customs and courtesy; and they would learn how the Army and the Army Nurse Corps were organized. Their classroom after today would be an empty Army hospital ward.

"Class dismissed," shouted the instructor over the bugles and the drums. They dashed off to Nurses' Mess, with the deafening clamor of the bugles replaced by the thunder of cannon.

Armed with this knowledge, and fortified by a whopping noon dinner, Cherry rushed out to collide with Sergeant Deake.

Sergeant Deake lined up the girls on the drill ground. It was the last week in September, but the afternoon sun was hot. They marched, perspiring and grim, in their dust-colored coveralls, as the hard-bitten little man screamed orders at them despairingly.

"No, *no*, NO! You start with your *left* foot—doncha know your own left foot, Miss?"

"Not Miss—Lieutenant!" redheaded Gwen Jones snapped back.

Sergeant Deake mopped his leathery face and neck. "Did I ask to train my superior officers? Did I? Not in all my twenty years in the Army! And females I'm stuck with—females!" he complained. "S'no use, but try it again. Forward, *march! Hut*-tup-thrip-four!"

They marched off in a straggly line, with about as much rhythm as a broken-down jalopy lurching along.

"Holy fried frogs!" Sergeant Deake yelled at them. "Don't go climbing up each other's heels—it wears out your shoes! Now try to keep together, nitwi—ladies—try!" he exhorted them contemptuously. "Count cadence, *count!*"

Dripping, breathless, torn between fury and giggles, they marched around and around the field, counting aloud. Cherry's back itched furiously. She dared not do anything about it, except wiggle a bit.

"Detail, halt! Fall out for a ten-minute break. You with the red cheeks! What do you think you're doing—dancing? Maybe I better get you a band!" he shouted.

Cherry whirled. "Try to be civil, lovey! I'm doing my best!"

"Lovey!" someone hooted derisively.

"Lovey!" someone else echoed. Laughingly, it spread through their ranks, "Hi, Sergeant Lovey!" "Lovey, our commander!" "Go on, order us around, Lovey, we love it!"

The wiry little man glared his best, especially at Cherry. He seemed really to dislike them. Sergeant Isaiah Deake, tough top-kick, who neither liked nor understood women, who loved the Army as a male hide-out from women, who regarded all women here as intruders, nuisances, and nitwits, was henceforth known as Lovey, the ladies' pet.

Late that night, after further wear and tear, Cherry was sure she would never walk again, but the next morning she was as good as new, even her feet. Unsuspecting, the girls all devoured an enormous breakfast and trustfully started in trucks for the drill ground.

They saw Sergeant Deake's gnarled figure waiting for them on the field. When the half-dozen boys who drove the trucks all sweetly called out to him, " 'Morning, Lovey!" a fierce glint came into his eyes.

"Let's see you march—if possible. Detail, 'ten-*tion!* Forward, *march! Hut*-tup-thrip-four! By the right flank—"

They marched like seasoned soldiers. Their lines were straight and evenly spaced, their steps aligned. The girls swung along straight-backed, with verve and the hint of a grin. Sergeant Deake's eyes bugged out. Cherry did not feel it was worth while to mention to him that they had drilled for hours last night, by flashlight, of their own accord, with her idea of a march on the victrola for inspiration.

"Detail, halt!" he got out feebly at last. "What came over you?"

There was a stirring in the ranks, like suppressed laughter. Apparently Sergeant Deake had not yet learned that nurses were veterans at discipline long before they entered the Army.

"Now will you love us, Lovey?" someone hidden in back called out.

"I'll never love you!" the sergeant barked at them. "And I'll be obliged to you not to love me! Love! Love in the Army! Great shades of Hannibal's elephants! I'm your commanding officer!"

Cherry raised her eyebrows. "So Lovey doesn't want us to love him," she grinned to herself. "He wants to be only our commanding officer." She tucked that information away for further, and devilish, use.

"You females are so smart, are you?" Sergeant Deake shouted. The man was unconvinced. "All right, let's see you perform some other tricks!"

Cherry was not prepared for the tricks Sergeant Deake pulled out of his bag. When he marched them down to a high wall, covered with nets, she shuddered.

"Get up there," he ordered them, "and climb down. That's the side of a ship and those are landing nets. You're climbing down into the water. Now, you know-it-all women, climb!"

Cherry climbed up a ladder to get to the dizzy height of the "ship," then monkey-wise worked her hands and feet into the net. It was a long way down to the hard ground below, thirty feet, and in the middle of it the nets started to sway alarmingly. It was Sergeant Deake, tugging at the nets, for realism and for sheer meanness.

"Ahoy for our good ship *Seasick!*" Cherry yelled out to her classmates.

Plump Bertha Larsen was having hard going, and Josie clung to the nets, terrified. But no one took a tumble. When they all "went ashore" safely, Lovey was not at all proud of his "females."

"See, nurses can do anything," they told him airily, mopping their faces.

"Bah!" Sergeant Deake spluttered. "I wash my hands of you! Let Lieutenant Graham handle you wild Injuns! Females in the Army! Let me work with real soldiers who have some respect for their commander! You're a waste of time!"

So the next day, the girls were confronted by a formal young man who was their superior officer. There was no fooling with him. When Lieutenant Graham explained gas mask drill, no one felt much like fooling, anyway. The nurses stood in rows on the grass, dressed for this drill in their white uniforms. Each girl wore on her heavy belt a gas mask in a carrier held in place by a strap over the right shoulder. Cherry found that it took concentration and perfectly co-ordinated movements to get those masks on in the space of seconds. But with practice, they were mastering it. The young lieutenant had them sniff "sniff sets"—bottles containing the identifying odors of lewisite and mustard and other gasses. It left them choking and impressed. Neither the gasses nor the young lieutenant was much fun. Next day, the girls were glad to see that Sergeant Deake was, resignedly, back again.

"Look at you!" he said gloomily, as they lined up before him. "Fatigues and curls! Field boots and—pink nail polish!" He eyed Cherry. He still had not forgiven her for the nickname she had tagged onto him.

Their feud grew livelier, day by day, into the second week of training. Cherry wondered what Lovey could possibly think up next. Sergeant Deake had them dive into foxholes and slit trenches; march along a road, then run for cover in the woods, throwing themselves flat; crawl cautiously on their hands and knees searching for booby traps; wiggle through mud and plow through sandy marshes. They certainly were learning how to take care of themselves, getting ready for anything, anywhere.

"We're doing all this," Cherry panted to him during their ten-minute rest period, pushing her black curls out of her eyes, "only because we want to win your praise, Lovey!" He turned scarlet.

The truth was, the nurses made good soldiers. They felt a real group spirit and group pride in their platoon's progress. But the better they did, the less Sergeant Deake gave them credit for and the less he liked them. "But we admire you," Gwen teased him, and Vivian tucked her camera in the huge catch-all pocket of her coveralls one day and snapped a picture of him, to his chagrin.

The crisis came when Sergeant Deake had to teach them something about camouflage. The girls stood in the sun and wind, watching him, and grinning. "You take your helmet," he shouted, taking off his own heavy metal helmet, which was covered with net. "Then you pick some leaves, like this. Then you stick the leaves in the net and kinda fix it up. Then you put your helmet on, see? Now nobody'd know it was you—you're disguised as a tree!"

They howled. Cherry could not resist calling out, "We'd know it was you!"

"What a stylish leafy bonnet!" Gwen teased.

"Thanks for the style notes, Lovey!"

Sergeant Deake exploded. For punishment, he drilled them and then took them on an eight-mile hike. They almost regretted the joke, but not quite.

" 'Night, Lovey!" Cherry called, unsquelched, as she staggered off the field. "See you tomorrow in that helmet!"

"I'll see *you* at inspection of quarters next Saturday morning!" Sergeant Deake promised her ferociously.

Cherry dropped on her bed after supper, heavy boots and all. A message said Captain Upham had phoned. But Cherry was too tired to call back. No time to see him anyway. There was a knock and Vivian Warren wearily came in from the room next door.

"Oh!" Vivian moaned. "My feet! My legs!" She dropped onto the bed alongside Cherry. "I'm so tired I don't even wish I could see Paul Endicott."

"Hi," Cherry said weakly, moving over an inch or so. "My feet are all beat-up too. Darn that Deake. But someone else is getting just as rugged a medical-and-basic workout as we are, so cheer up."

"You mean the enlisted men who are going to be medical corpsmen? What befalls them?"

"Plenty. I read in the Manual, Cherry said virtuously, "that they get thirteen weeks of basic training in Medical Department techniques, first aid and ward stuff. Then we nurses teach them some more when they come to help us on the wards. There's about seventy or eighty boys here in the Hospital Corps School. Poor things." She rubbed her knees tenderly.

"Uh-huh." Vivian yawned, and fished in her pocket. "Tired as I am, I stopped off at the PX to get this. Look. It's priceless."

She held out a snapshot of Sergeant Deake. There he was as Vivian had snapped him in the midst of an anti-female rage, arms upheld, mouth open, his cap crooked.

Cherry looked at the snapshot speculatively for a while. The corners of her red mouth began to turn up. "Do you suppose we could get sixty copies of this made by Saturday morning?"

"I guess so. But why?"

"Wait," Cherry said. With a supreme effort, she rolled herself off the bed and made for the door. "Council of war. Our platoon vs. Woman-hater Lovey," she explained briefly to Vivian. "Come on!"

They started down the hall, knocking on each door. As Cherry confided her plan, the girls forgot their fatigue and the third floor of Nurses' Quarters whooped with laughter long after lights out.

They needed laughter, for the last few days of Sergeant Deake's field training grew tougher and tougher. The worst, the infiltration course, came on Friday. Sergeant Deake led them to a muddy exposed field, without trees or shelter of any kind, strung with barbed wire, full of shell holes and ditches.

"You've got to get across that field with full first-aid musette bag," he ordered them. "There are wounded soldiers on the other side and they need you. Look out for the machine-gun bullets!" There was an ominous whining sound and a crash. Sergeant Deake jumped close to the truck, the girls threw themselves flat. He added, yelling over the biting rat-tat-tat of thirty-caliber machine guns from the woods:

"*Those are live bullets!* Now get across that field!" It was an order and a dare.

Cherry lay flat on her stomach, petrified with fear. Then she started to crawl, cautiously, hugging the ground, as she had been taught. Bullets sprayed only thirty inches above her. She dared not raise her head. She slipped and rolled into a shell hole. For a moment, she lay there taut, face down, fingers and toes dug into the mud.

Cherry listened breathlessly to TNT charges heavily exploding on the course. Mortar and cannon shells would blast like that in actual battle. Her stomach sank as the control tower detonated dynamite—right to the side of her! The earth shook, smoke whirled in the shaken air.

She was quivering and clammy and exhausted and clung flat to the earth, trembling with fright. She was so scared her legs would not go. But here came the sickening rat-tat-tat of machine-gun bullets pursuing her. Panic-stricken, Cherry suddenly wanted to stand up and run. But bullets would surely hit her if she stood up! In fright she started to crawl again, to crawl away from that whistle of bullets slashing through the air. She was gasping and her heart was pounding, but she did move forward! More TNT roared and thundered as it exploded. She had gained two yards.

She had to get to those imaginary wounded soldiers. Every second counted if their lives were to be saved. Cherry crawled, getting her coveralls caught in barbed wire once, once cutting her hand on a stone, but she crawled. After a lifetime under a staring sun, as nakedly exposed as a fly, she crawled under the final barbed wire. She had made it!

Not even when every last girl successfully had crossed that terrible barrier did Lovey have a kind word for them. Lieutenant Graham later that day publicly complimented Cherry's platoon on crossing the field under fire, and in a shorter time than men soldiers at the same stage of training. The Commanding Officer—the Old Man himself—sent her platoon a commendation.

"But not Lovey! Oh, no, not Lovey!" Cherry said at supper, half-amused, half-exasperated. "Just wait till tomorrow morning inspection!"

Saturday morning came, and with it came tough Sergeant Deake to Nurses' Quarters for the rigid weekly inspection. Preceding Sergeant Deake were Colonel Wylie, Captain Endicott, and Lieutenant Graham. Sergeant Deake and Captain Endicott wore white cotton gloves with which to run a finger along shelves and under beds to find any trace of dust. Usually any soldier in his right mind dreads inspection. But this Saturday morning the girls lined up happily, each before the opened door of her room. Cherry had a hard time making her face behave. Sergeant Deake and the officers stepped into the first room. It was quiet little Mai Lee's room.

There was a grunt, then a pause. Sergeant Deake's eye apparently had fallen on the raging snapshot of himself, pinned up over Mai Lee's dresser. The faces of the other three men were carefully expressionless. Sergeant Deake stepped into the room across the hall, past dignified Marie Swift. Cherry heard another peculiar noise. No doubt Sergeant Lovey had seen the same snapshot of himself, tacked up over Marie's dresser. Sergeant Deake and his party progressed down the hall. His leathery face grew redder and redder. In each of the sixty girls' rooms that awful snapshot of himself hung loyally over the dresser. In Cherry's room, it was further adorned by a fresh red rose sentimentally draped over it.

Colonel Wylie looked stern. Young Lieutenant Graham's expression was stern, too, but obviously controlled. Captain Endicott, stiff as a martinet, glowered disapproval. At the end of the hall, Sergeant Deake looked as if he wanted to flee.

"Nurses!" Colonel Wylie's shout broke the uncomfortable silence. "What is the meaning of this impertinence? Explain!"

The girls stood at beautiful attention. Colonel Wylie's angry eye fell, by force of habit, on Cherry.

"Lieutenant Ames! What did *you* have to do with this . . . this slander?"

Cherry replied respectfully, "We prefer not to think of it as slander, sir. In fact, sir, we think of it as a tribute. Sergeant Deake is our standard of a soldier and a man!"

This time Sergeant Deake turned pale. Lieutenant Graham hastily disappeared. Colonel Wylie gave the girls a rapid bawling-out. Then he turned and marched out in disgust, with Captain Endicott at his heels, and Sergeant Deake bringing up the rear.

The girls relaxed and melted into giggles. Everyone immediately tried to crowd into Cherry's room. She was hanging precariously out the window, making frantic motions for them to keep still. Down on the porch, Sergeant Deake was talking to Lieutenant Graham. The men's flustered voices floated up to the eavesdropping girls.

"Do you really think," Lovey was asking hoarsely and earnestly, "that they really admire me and look up to me?"

"Er—why—" it was Lieutenant Graham's embarrassed voice now, "why, of course they do! There's not a doubt of it!"

"Well, what do you know about that!" They heard Sergeant Deake's low, gratified whistle. "And after the hard-boiled way I treated them! And I'm their ideal of a soldier and a man! I guess women aren't so bad at that!"

The girls doubled up and clasped their hands over their mouths, nearly exploding with suppressed mirth. Cherry almost fell out the window as she watched Sergeant Deake strut away across the Post, his tough wiry figure stiff and pompous with pride.

Cherry turned back into the room, choking with laughter. "We cured him, all right! But I think—" she collapsed onto a chair and gasped out, "—I think—the joke's—on *us!*"

CHAPTER IV

Cherry Meets Bunce

CHERRY APPRECIATED HER OLIVE DRAB CAPE THIS CRISP October morning. She drew it more closely about her as she trotted across the windy Post toward the station hospital, one hand hanging on to her starched white nurse's cap. This was the morning she braved Army wards, soldier patients, corpsmen, and any other brand-new terrors which might turn up. She already was halfway through her month's training, a two weeks' veteran. But as she hastened down the quiet hospital street, hoping to arrive at Ward 2 approximately on time, Cherry's assurance melted away like ice cream under a puppy's tongue. After all, this was her very first professional nursing!

She wandered into a sort of tunnel connecting the twelve ward buildings, then into an anteroom marked

W–2. There was no one in the room; a wall clock ticked loudly and accusingly.

"Lieutenant Ames, you're late!" Cherry jumped and saw the Ward Officer striding toward her. "Lateness is not tolerated in the Army! Sign in in red."

Cherry knew her face was as red as the ink. "This is a pretty start," she thought. "Here's where I reform."

Just then an extraordinarily tall and youthful soldier, wearing a Red Cross arm band, ambled in. "Clock's fast, sir," he said. He reached up and nonchalantly shoved the minute hand back five minutes. He grinned amiably at Cherry and shuffled past her. Cherry dared not smile back, for the Ward Officer, consulting his own wrist watch, was rather crossly holding out the book for her to sign in in black. Saved! Who was that tall youngster?

She found him a few moments later when the night nurse showed her around. There was no mistaking, even at a distance, that tall stumbling figure whose khaki clothes hung loosely. The boy—he was a corpsman— was bending over a patient with clumsy tenderness. Cherry whispered to the nurse, "Who's that?"

The nurse followed Cherry's dark gaze. "Bunce Smith. He's my best corpsman, but he just got off scrubbing detail again. Now, the ward is laid out like this——"

"Why was he on scrubbing detail?" Cherry persisted in a whisper.

"Oh, Bunce can't keep out of trouble. This time he referred to one of the superior officers as an underdone egg and when they put him on K.P. for punishment, he carved his initials into all the potatoes. The ward is arranged," the nurse said firmly, "on this plan—" And Cherry obediently followed her.

Along this short wooden corridor were several tiny service rooms: kitchen, utility room, lavatories, doctor's examining room, and nurses' office. This led them directly into the ward itself—a big, long, low room with rough wood walls, lots of windows, and rows and rows of white iron beds. Thirty pairs of inquisitive masculine eyes turned on Cherry. She grinned back uncertainly as the nurse swept her down the row of beds to show her the two sun porches. The soldiers watched the new nurse with interest. Cherry suspected that the moment she was left here alone their teasing would begin. But the nurse was describing the various cases and showing her the charts: colds, a sore throat, poison ivy, two badly upset stomachs, a burn.

"The corpsmen will tell you the details and give you any help you want." The nurse mentioned Cherry's name and the corpsmen's names. Half a dozen young men looked up from their bedside tasks to smile at

Cherry. Cherry smiled back at the corpsmen hopefully and rather desperately. Bunce beamed.

"Good-by, Lieutenant Ames," the nurse said. "And—er—good luck." She went off, leaving Cherry on her own, with thirty-six lively young men to cope with. "Good luck, huh?" Cherry thought. "I'll need it!"

Assuming her most professional air, Cherry looked down at her record book for guidance. It read:

> 7:30 A.M. Arrive on duty. Check temperatures, order diets, check foods sent over from mess kitchen, visit any new or very ill patient before doctor's sick call.

Cherry decided to plunge into these tasks at once to forestall the teasing. Armed with her thermometer, she started with the first bed.

"We already took temperatures, ma'am," proudly said a quiet-looking corpsman. "And see, we dusted and got the beds in alignment and the floor's just been washed."

"Yes, ma'am," said another corpsmen, coming up eagerly, "everything's all done for you!"

Cherry tried to look official as she put away her thermometer. The whole ward was listening. "I'll just go check up in the kitchen," she said hastily.

"Oh, that's okay, ma'am," said Bunce, stumbling over his own feet. "We checked. The fluids for the day came over and we've got the other food in the hot water tables. Breakfast was an hour ago. Don't you bother. We'll do things for you."

"Well, thank you, and in that case," Cherry said uncertainly, "I'll have a look at the more seriously ill patients."

"Shucks," said Bunce, vigorously chewing a wad of gum, "no one seriously sick here."

Cherry looked desperate. She could not just stand around before these three dozen pairs of eyes, not knowing where to start on her job! From one of the beds, a boy sang out:

"I'll tell you what you can do, Nurse! Come and hold my hand!"

Cherry flushed. The teasing was good-humored but, as nurse in charge, she had to maintain discipline.

"The hand-holding department is out to lunch!" she retorted.

There was a roar of approving laughter. Another boy sat up against his pillow and teased, "Oh, Nurse! I'm so-o-o sick! Please help me!"

"Why, certainly," Cherry said and started briskly for his bed, snatching up an ominous-looking bottle of medicine and some rubber tubing on her way. The boy abruptly sobered. There was another wave of laughter.

"Okay, Nurse," someone said good-naturedly. "Now we know who's boss!"

"And a good thing for you that you learn fast," Cherry joked back. The boys were smiling at her now, to her great relief. One of the corpsmen came to her further rescue by saying:

"There's a burn here . . . we don't know exactly how to . . . I mean, would you . . . ?"

Cherry took charge of the burn. Then there were throats to be swabbed. The soldiers were both game and grateful for the smallest help. It was almost time for the ward doctor's visit when Cherry reached the last bed. A sharp-eyed young man with a sickly mustache caught Cherry's hand.

"Got a minue to talk to me, Beautiful?" he inquired. Cherry did not like his cocky manner.

"What do you want?" she asked. She glanced at him professionally, then at his chart. The corpsmen seemed to be taking proper care of him.

"I'm lonesome, Beautiful." He hung onto her hand.

"The name is Lieutenant Ames. And I'm busy." Cherry tried to tug free but he held on, very much pleased with himself. She could see angry glances from the near-by beds. "Let go!" she said, annoyed.

The young man with the mustache laughed. Cherry felt her cheeks growing redder than ever.

Just then big Bunce lumbered up with a threatening look on his face. The patient let go of Cherry's hand in a hurry.

"I'll smack you from here to Oshkosh," Bunce muttered.

"Bunce!" Cherry remonstrated under her breath, drawing the boy into the corridor out of sight of curious eyes. "You must never smack—er, hit a patient!"

"I'm sorry, sir—I mean, ma'am—Lieuten—Miss Ames—oh, gosh! Out of every five hundred nice guys in the Army, there's only about one lug. And," he said firmly, from his lanky six-foot-three, "I wish I could smack this one!"

Cherry repressed a smile. Bunce was very earnest, big and awkward, and so young she wondered how this "kid brother" had got into the Army. His light brown hair curled up at the ends, and his slow grin and that chewing gum apparently were perpetual. She said as sternly as she could:

"Didn't you have any training for ward nursing?"

Bunce shifted from one large foot to the other and hitched up his trousers. " 'Course I had training. Best corpsman in the class. Take a pride in my work. As a matter of fact, I used to want to be a doctor." His voice was so plaintive it made Cherry curious.

"Don't you want to be a doctor any more?"

"Well, you see, ma'am, after my father died I took care of Mom and my two kid brothers. Worked on farms around my town, mostly. I finished high school, but a doctor needs—oh, darn. Might as well forget it."

Cherry looked at him with sympathy in her big dark eyes. She understood about that deep and exciting urge to save lives. To cheer him up, she asked, "Where'd you get your name, Bunce?"

The grin returned. He took another chew on his gum and yanked his khaki shirt into place. "Well, I expect I was such a bouncin' baby they just had to call me Bounce. Bounce—Bunce—you know, two for a nickel, four for a dime"—his feet had started of their own accord to beat out a tap rhythm—"Bunce got a haircut just, like mine!" he wound up joyously. "Say, Miss Cherry, you just let me know when you want anyone smacked!"

Cherry gravely agreed to notify him. Just then a door flew open, and an attractive nurse in crisp white hurried in.

"Lieutenant Ames? I'm the head nurse on these wards. The doctor's coming right in. He's new. And I hear," her voice dropped to a warning whisper, "that he's a terror! His name is Captain Upham." She suddenly assumed a dazzling smile and held the door open for Lex.

Lex gave her a shrewd, distrustful look as he marched in. The head nurse left with a shrug. Then Lex saw Cherry and relaxed.

"Where in thunder have you been these last two weeks?" he said happily under his breath. Lex looked imposing in his uniform, solid, and very capable. His golden-brown eyes, under the strikingly dark, decided brows, swept around the ward, seeing everything. His purposeful face tightened a little. "Any complications with Private D'Agostino? Are you keeping Lane on isolation?" he shot at her. "How are the colds coming along? There's an epidemic of virus pneumonia in a near-by city, watch those colds, Cherry—Nurse."

"Yes, sir," Cherry said, happy to be working with Lex again. They went from bed to bed. Lex demanded reports, examined, prescribed, ordered new diets. Lex might be a brilliant terror to the staff, but to the patients he was kindness and gentleness itself. Cherry could see that the boys liked and trusted him.

Just as Cherry and Lex were helping a soldier back into bed after a treatment, Captain Endicott entered. He swung down the ward, a sleek stiff figure beside the casually clad soldiers in their gray Army pajamas and maroon robes. When he saw who the nurse was, he smiled in surprise.

"Good morning, Lieutenant Ames! I've been wondering when I'd see you."

"I've been wondering the same thing," Lex said in a faintly warning tone.

"Hope you don't mind my barging in on your precincts like this," Captain Endicott said. "I've come to see Private Trent from L Company."

Cherry said impulsively, "It's nice of you to visit the men when they're sick."

Captain Endicott said dryly, "As a matter of fact, I'm here to check on just how sick Trent really is." He looked down at the boy they had just helped back to bed. Trent, who had been through a drastic treatment, was pale and exhausted. "Hmm," said Endicott.

Lex said sharply, "This boy is not shamming. You will receive a report on his condition." He stuffed his stethoscope back in his pocket. "And now, Captain Endicott, if your business here is finished——"

Cherry wished Lex would not always be so brusque. But as a matter of fact, Captain Endicott was holding up the many treatments and prescriptions Lex still had to give. And she herself was in a hurry to get this patient a cup of strong, hot tea to brace him up.

Paul Endicott, offended, turned to go, and collided with Bunce. Bunce was sprinting along with a cup of tea—for Trent, Cherry realized gratefully. A drop or two of the tea splashed on Captain Endicott's immaculate pinks.

"Sorry, sir," said Bunce and intently went on to the patient. Cherry saw Lex's approving nod. She wondered exactly what it was that Lex approved.

Captain Endicott wiped his trouser knee, frowning. Cherry apologized for her corpsman.

"Quite all right, though I think Private Smith might apologize for himself." He glanced critically at the boy.

Bunce looked up from the bedside. "I did say I'm sorry, sir."

"Perhaps we have some spot remover," Cherry said hastily. Endicott was still fussing with his handkerchief over the tiny spots of tea.

"Good-by, Captain Endicott," Lex said deliberately, and stood there waiting for him to leave the ward.

Paul Endicott glared at all three of them and departed.

Cherry relaxed and returned to work. For the rest of that day, growing more tired but less bewildered, Cherry filled out reports, saw to the X-ray and laboratory tests which Dr. Upham had ordered, supervised the corpsmen who gave simple treatments and morning care, checked the medicine cabinet, accompanied the terrifying Chief Nurse on her inspection visit, kept an eye on the diet kitchen at lunchtime, bolted her own lunch, visited a new patient, gave more treatments, attended another doctor on the two-thirty sick call, and at long last, at three-thirty, turned over the day report book to the afternoon nurse. Cherry felt by three-thirty that it was at least next week. And Thursday, her free day, seemed two years off.

Thursday finally arrived. Cherry spent the morning blissfully sleeping. In the afternoon, she loafed at Nurses' Quarters with some of her friends who also had the day off. The girls were upstairs, congregated in

Cherry's room, trying on their new uniforms, and laughing their heads off at the way some of them fit— or failed to fit.

Gwen waddled around the room, duck fashion, to show how the back of her jacket bounced up like a tail, instead of lying flat. "Meet Gwen Quack Jones!" she said, waggling her coattail and clumping about in Bertha Larsen's shoes, two sizes too big for her.

"That's nothing, look at me!" Bertha panted from the doorway. "I'm a—a sausage!" Plump Bertha's uniform was so tight she could scarcely breathe.

"Come in and sit down!" they invited her.

Bertha looked scared. "I wouldn't dare sit down in this—this——"

Cherry, Vivian and Ann sat on the bed, rocking against one another with laughter.

"How's this, girls?" Cherry said. She took a deep breath, held it, buttoned the top button of her high-necked shirt and looked cross-eyed.

"You ought to have your picture taken that way!" Vivian cried and unbuttoned Cherry's tight collar.

Ann took out her sewing box, but no one wanted to be sensible. Gwen was still quacking and waggling her way around the room, gibbering furious nonsense à la Donald Duck. When the phone rang, they were too weak with laughter to answer it. Finally Cherry pulled herself together and said, "Hello!"

The clerk's voice, choked from a cold and further strangled by a buzzing wire, said what sounded like "Laptin Edicod to zee Bis Warren."

"Miss Rabbit Warren?" Cherry inquired into the phone, and the girls exploded.

There was an offended silence at the other end of the crackling wire, then the indignant clerk said, "Bis *Litian* Warren." And the clerk hung up.

Cherry held her nose and repeated the announcement. The other girls sang out, "Oh-h-h, Vivian, your heart throb's waiting downstairs!" "Warren's got a bad case of it!"

Vivian's pale face flushed shell pink, but she accepted the teasing with good grace. Cherry was relieved to note that.

"You come too!" Vivian seized Cherry's hand. With the other hand, Vivian was nervously smoothing her light brown hair and patting her uniform into place.

"You don't want a third person along!" Cherry protested.

"You mustn't stay long!" Vivian warned her. She was tugging Cherry along the hall to the stairs. "I just want you to come down and say how-do-you-do and show Paul that you really do like him." Cherry heard that with mixed feelings.

"You don't like Paul very much, do you?"

Cherry replied uneasily, "Oh, I'm not much for handsome men."

"It's only because you don't know Paul!" Vivian pleaded, "Stay for a while."

When they entered the sitting room of Nurses' Quarters and Cherry saw how Vivian's soft hazel eyes shone, and how eager she was to have Cherry like her beau, Cherry softened. Perhaps she had been unfair or too hasty in judging Endicott. She was concerned, too, to learn how Endicott treated her friend Vivian. So she said a friendly hello to the sleek, handsome young man who rose to greet them, and tried to look at him without prejudice.

"How lucky I am, with *two* girls to talk to!" Captain Endicott smiled, as the three of them sat down on a big couch.

Vivian said shyly, "It's high time my two favorite people became acquainted."

Paul Endicott's gray eyes expressed his appreciation of the compliment, and he said, "How would you suggest going about it? Shall I tell you my life story?" he said lightly.

Cherry thought he was joking. But Captain Endicott was not at all loath to make an audience of two pretty and attentive girls. He told them about himself, at some length. He was the only son of wealthy parents and he admitted, with an engaging smile, that he was badly spoiled. He talked so much that Cherry began to wonder how she could break away. She knew she was tactlessly staying too long: Vivian's big soft eyes, past Paul's blond head, implored her to go. But Paul Endicott talked on.

"As a matter of fact," he continued persuasively, "the only job my father would hear of my holding for long was a position with my uncle. Believe me, I'd much rather have been working, like other men, instead of traveling around." Cherry was not persuaded. He had lived in London, Paris, Rome, Cairo, Rio—he had seen, enjoyed, done everything. No wonder, Cherry thought, Vivian is impressed. As Paul stopped for breath, Cherry rose to her feet.

"I'm enjoying this so much. I do hate to leave, but I'm afraid I've things to do. So if you will excuse me, I'll run along."

She saw Vivian's eager face, silently asking if Cherry did not like Paul better, now that she knew more about him. But Paul's talk had confirmed Cherry in her opinion that he was a vain and shallow and selfish man. She could find just one big point in his favor: it was generally acknowledged that he was a conscientious and competent officer . . . a rather self-important, over-bearing officer . . . but he did do his job well. She tried to hide these doubtful thoughts from Vivian's trusting gaze and turned to leave. Some day, preferably soon, she would talk to Vivian about Endicott. But it would be difficult, Vivian was falling in love with him, and Cherry knew she was going to put off the talk as long as possible.

Cherry went back upstairs to the nurses' dubious fashion show.

The girls were in the process of trying out new hairdo's on one another, with some wild and startling results, when Vivian returned almost two hours later. She strolled into the crowded room, dreamy-eyed.

"It's a wonder you don't go bumping into things, with all those stars in your eyes!" Gwen declared.

"How was the dream prince?" they all demanded.

Vivian sighed. Then she grinned back at them. "All right, all right! I might as well tell you kids at once, before you worm it out of me. We took a walk around Post and then we stopped at the Officers' Club and then Paul," she said tenderly, "bought me a soda!"

The girls pretended to swoon. Cherry, more sympathetic than the others, gently ribbed Vivian, "It sounds very romantic."

"It was," Vivian replied solemnly.

"A soda!" Marie Swift echoed in ecstatic tones. "Honey flavor, wasn't it?"

"Roses and—and perfume," Vivian gulped. But she could laugh now and take the teasing well, instead of fearing and mistrusting the other girls for it, as she once had. What a change in Vivian's character! What a happy change! Cherry thought, "Here's hoping nothing—and no one—hurts Vivian again."

Vivian turned confidingly to Cherry. "And you know what else? There's a dance at the Officers' Country Club this Saturday evening and Paul asked me to go with him!" She was glowing with happiness. "Cherry, you're going with Lex, I suppose. Why don't we make it a foursome?"

Cherry promised in some embarrassment to ask Lex about it when she saw him that evening. But when he asked her to go to the dance with him, she could not bring herself to mention Vivian's suggestion.

They had a fine, comfortable, openhearted time. They took the bus into town, found a good movie, and after that, food. Lex understood about Cherry's being hungry at all hours of the day and night. They squeezed into a booth in a Chinese restaurant and stuffed happily on chow mein. As they ate, they talked. Cherry thought Lex was the most satisfying person to talk to.

"Oh, by the way," Cherry said at last, "Vivian suggested that you and I, and Endicott and herself, make a foursome of it at the dance."

Lex groaned. "I don't want to go with that phony. Do you?"

"No, but I don't want to let Vivian down."

"We-ell," said Lex, "I don't want to see him make a fool of Vivian, either. But let's let the foursome business take care of itself."

Cherry took Lex's cue and changed the subject.

"How's Dr. Joe?" she asked. She did not see much of her old friend, now that he was assistant to Unit Director Wylie. "What's all the mystery?"

Lex scowled. "I—don't—know. Something awfully strange there. I can't figure it out. Dr. Fortune and Dr. Wylie are both acting like a couple of G-men."

Cherry laughed. "If there's a mystery, I'll dig it out sooner or later!"

Lex said seriously, "Watch your step! We'll be leaving here in about two weeks—sailing to ports unknown—all this hush stuff may come out sooner than you think. Promise me you'll be careful, Cherry. I know your talent for getting yourself into trouble!"

Cherry hastily changed the subject again. She asked Lex what he thought of the way she was running her Army ward.

"Not bad, Nurse, not bad at all," he grinned at her. "But I think a lot of the credit goes to that youngster—what's his name?—Bunce. He's a fine and serious corpsman, for all his wild ways. The Army is going to be hearing from him, I lay you a nickel."

"Your nickel is safe. But better not risk a nickel on me. You know, Lex," Cherry confided, leaning her chin on her hand, "I've got an awful lot of doubts about myself. About whether I'll make a good Army nurse, or whether I'll fail in some emergency. I wouldn't tell anyone else but you, but Lex—I'm still scared."

"Well, honey, who isn't? We're going to go through a trial by fire. At least we'll all go through it together."

"Lex, you're nice!" she said affectionately.

"I like you too!" Cherry and Lex sat there in the booth and beamed at each other.

Army nursing was not all romancing. Cherry worked hard in the following days. On the ward, Bunce did not make things any easier. Six soldiers had dared call him a bedpan warrior, and Bunce had gotten even, and thereby found himself put to scrubbing floors again. Cherry sympathized, but she had a difficult time without her most competent corpsman.

One morning on the way to their wards, Gwen reminded Cherry, "There's tennis, golf, swimming, dancing, cards, libraries—a grand garrison life here for us!"

Cherry noted with a grin that they were walking past Expectancy Ward, where soldiers' wives could have their babies at the cost of seventy cents. She replied, "Yes, but when? When do we play tennis, golf, et cetera?" Her world consisted only of these wards, X-ray, Pharmacy, Operating, Dispensary, Dental. "I never have time for fun," she mourned to Gwen, as she sprinted into her own Medical Ward.

Cherry walked miles and miles on duty. "I've figured out," she announced to Ann and Gwen at the end of the week, "that with all our hospital buildings stretched out flat as they are, and all connecting, they measure three whole miles! And Sergeant Deake is still putting us through some fancy paces! I won't have any feet left for the dance."

But Saturday evening found Cherry very fit for the dance. Donning her new dress uniform, gleaming with gold, put her in a gay mood. Vivian, in the next room, called out nonsense through their connecting door as she dressed. The fact that Paul Endicott was taking her to the dance, that this was her first Army dance and her first real beau, brought lights to Vivian's large hazel eyes and a lilt to her voice.

Cherry patted a last smidge of powder on her nose. Lex and Paul both were calling for the girls at nine. It was almost nine now! Then the downstairs desk phoned up to say "Dr. Upham is waiting." A moment later, the phone shrilled again, and Vivian dashed for the call.

Cherry flew down the stairs, black curls flying under her smart officer's cap, thinking, "Why did they have to arrive together!"

Both Paul and Lex were in their best uniforms. Lex looked imposing but Paul, his fair hair gleaming above a meticulous uniform, looked positively glamorous. As they stood side by side in the hall, their dislike of each other was unmistakable. A fine foursome they would make!

Cherry was just saying good evening to them when Vivian arrived. She looked pretty, but she betrayed her excitement and nervousness. When Endicott put a bunch of golden chrysanthemums into her hands, Vivian was speechless.

"You should always have lovely things," Endicott said. "Like flowers in your room."

Lex was laughing behind his eyes. While Vivian was asking Lieutenant Glenn to take care of her flowers, Lex looked at Cherry with a wicked twinkle, picked up an ash tray, and presented it to her with a gallant flourish. "Mademoiselle, allow me! This will lend your room glamour."

Paul Endicott looked offended. "Shall we start, Vivian?" Cherry and Lex were trying to hide their mirth. "Sorry I can't offer you two a lift," Endicott said, stalking away from Lex and Cherry. "Too bad you'll have to walk. I managed to get a jeep—*and* a driver."

"Walk, nothing!" Lex retorted in high good spirits. "Wait till you see *our* romantic chariot!"

It was a brand-new ambulance! Cherry and Lex clambered up to the seat, Lex slammed the door, and they were off to the dance with a wild clanging.

Jeep and ambulance bounced along the five miles down the road. When both couples drew up before the

Country Club, Vivian was gasping from her jeep ride. The wind had played havoc with her neat hair-do, and Paul's pride in his taxi was visibly dampened when he saw the state of his lady. Cherry felt a real satisfaction in their nice, comfortable ambulance as she smoothed Vivian's hair for her. Then the two couples walked up the gravel drive to the clubhouse.

Within was a gay scene. Uniforms, greens and pinks, mingled on the dance floor, before roaring fires in twin fireplaces, over tiny tables on the glassed-in terrace. A dance orchestra played at one end of the big room, and when they stopped, a rumba band at the other end of the big room, started up. The music was swollen by talk and laughter, tinkling glasses, the beat and shuffle of dancing feet. It was Cherry's first Army party and she found it dashingly formal and very gay.

Cherry danced the first dance with Lex, of course, and Vivian with Endicott. Then, with frigid politeness, Captain Endicott danced exactly one dance with Cherry, while Lex and Vivian whirled around the floor. Endicott returned Cherry to Lex as if she were an undesirable puppy he was handing over to its undesirable owner. For the rest of the evening, he carefully ignored them.

"It's too bad," Cherry whispered regretfully to Lex, "that the first personable man to pay Vivian any attention had to be Paul's type."

Lex nodded in silent agreement.

"It's so important for Vivian to find someone who'd be understanding and sympathetic, and Paul's so self-centered."

"Right you are," Lex agreed.

"He certainly doesn't care for us," she said, "or Bunce either."

"Never mind Endicott or Bunce," Lex said gruffly. "Let's enjoy ourselves."

It was a good party. They danced a long time, then strolled out to the terrace. They challenged "Ding" and Gwen to a fast game of backgammon. Later they joined a laughing, chatting group before a roaring fire.

Cherry thoroughly enjoyed herself. She almost succeeded, as Lex had suggested, in forgetting Endicott.

But Cherry wondered, as she sipped her punch and laughed with the others, if Endicott was really somebody who could be dismissed so easily.

CHAPTER V

~~~~~~

On Bivouac

"STEP ON IT!" SERGEANT DEAKE SHOUTED OVER THE heavy tramp of feet and rumble of gun caissons. "Only one little mile more! Then we bivouac! Ladies, you can't fail me now!"

Cherry sighed, shifted her heavy musette bag and her heavy helmet to more comfortable positions, and kept on plodding. They had been marching all morning and it was now early afternoon. All around her marched her fellow nurses, and ahead of them and behind them, endless columns of infantrymen and artillerymen. This was the long-awaited bivouac, grand wind-up of Cherry's training. Everyone wore a tan arm band. These warriors were the Tans; the eight hundred enemy Blues were advancing on another road. They were going to fight a simulated battle.

Some tank boys went roaring by on their enormous steel monster, which they had affectionately named Baby, raising clouds of dust. Cherry swallowed the dust, wet her dry lips, and looked longingly at a roadside stand before a farmhouse. It was piled high with glass jugs of rosy liquid and the sign read: "Ice cold cherry cider—All you can drink—Ten cents." Right in front of the stand, Sergeant Deake, in response to a hand signal from up the line, yelled, "Detail, halt!" Up and down the road, the order was signaled and repeated, and the long winding line came to a stop.

"Yoo-hoo, Sergeant Deake!" Cherry yelled, as respectfully as is possible at the top of one's lungs.

He fell behind to Cherry's column. "You want something, Miss Ames?"

"Yes!" Cherry said. She shook dust off her field coveralls. "I want a drink. Over there."

Sergeant Deake looked at her reproachfully. "D'you think the Commanding Officer's going to let you break ranks for refreshments? Maybe you'd like a taxi? Honestly, Lieutenant Ames, I'm surprised at you." Cherry had to smile at his softened manner. "Don't let me catch you taking a drink out of your canteen, either. Not after all this sun and exercise."

Cherry was about to mutter that she did not want lukewarm water anyhow, when Captain Endicott rode up beside the nurses' ranks. He halted his jeep and spoke at length to Sergeant Deake.

Just then the farmhouse door flew open and a little girl of about ten, with fair sunburned hair, came running out. She was crying and there was a bloodstain on her faded cotton dress. She stumbled as she ran toward the road. Suddenly she stopped and stared at the Red Cross arm band.

"You're nurses, aren't you?" she cried in a thin little voice. "You *are* nurses—please somebody help my little brother——"

Cherry and the other nurses looked at the frightened child in concern. But Cherry, like the others, hesitated to act outside of her Army duties—especially with Captain Endicott watching coldly. "Oh, please!" the little girl begged. "Can't you help my little brother?"

"What's wrong?" Cherry asked her gently.

"Jack—he—we were out by the silo playing on the corn cutter—and Jack, he's only four, he didn't know any better—he got his arm cut! And he's—" the child's face screwed up as she wordlessly held out her stained dress. "Please come! Somebody come!"

Cherry looked around for Sergeant Deake. This was a ten-minute break and Sergeant Deake would be generous enough to relax the rules and let her go for five minutes. But Sergeant Deake had gone up the line. Only Paul Endicott was here, sitting stiffly in his jeep.

"May I leave for five minutes, sir?" Cherry asked him.

"Certainly not."

"But this child needs——"

"I heard her, Lieutenant Ames. Let her call a doctor."

The child, clinging to Cherry's side, cried. "We—we haven't any telephone! And anyway, our Dr. Gillis in Milltown is in the Army and went away. And Pop hasn't enough gasoline to drive all the way to Center City to——"

"That's too bad, but it's not our concern," Paul Endicott interrupted. "This is not a civilian nursing corps."

Cherry managed to keep her voice calm. "Captain Endicott, I could give first aid in five minutes—three minutes!"

"No."

Cherry blew out an angry breath, then looked down at the anxious child.

"What's your name, dear?"

"Sally. And my mother's in the hospital!"

"Well, Sally, you tell me about Jack's arm."

Sally described her brother's wound as well as she was able.

"All right," Cherry said soothingly. "Here is what you must do." And she explained, very clearly and carefully, how to stop the bleeding, how to clean the wound and bandage it. "Do you understand now? Good, you're a brave girl. I know you can take care of your brother," she reassured her.

But Sally, though calmer now, was still badly frightened. Cherry glanced at the name on the mailbox: Johnson. They were farmers, without a phone or gasoline or much money. Cherry realized that no distant doctor would be summoned to treat the boy. The sister's first aid would not be adequate. She made an instant, reckless decision, not with her mind but with her heart. Dropping her voice very low because Paul was suspiciously listening, she said, "You do what I said and I'll come back tonight and take care of Jack."

"You will do nothing of the sort!" Captain Endicott snapped out. So he had heard! "I expressly forbid you to leave the Army area for any such purpose!"

Sally's worried face clouded again and she looked up at Cherry with unhappy eyes. Cherry's fingers tightened around the small shoulder. She determined, Endicott or no Endicott, broken rules or no broken rules, to get back to these children tonight! The little boy needed help! Especially with his mother away. And Cherry was not going to let that four-year-old risk a serious infection for the sake of a petty taskmaster like Paul Endicott!

The column started off again, and Cherry marched away reluctantly with her platoon of nurses. She felt Sally's pleading eyes following her. But she had to trudge on, a part of that long, winding, tramping column of soldiers under full pack.

"I'd better think of something cheerful," Cherry decided, "and stop this useless brooding about those children." She looked at Gwen and Ann at either side of her to see if they felt like talking. But the nurses had long since given up chattering and singing to save breath. "Let's see. What's cheering, besides cherry cider?" Lex might be cheering, except that she had been too busy to see him since the dance. Lex was along today, and Captain Endicott was present as Liaison Officer to the Commanding Officer, she had heard, whatever that meant. Her monthly pay was cheering— one hundred and fifty dollars base pay plus all living expenses paid for her. Tonight's "battle" with her own Tans fighting the Blues might prove pretty exciting. Cherry was a little vague as to the military techniques involved, except that there was going to be a lot of shooting and spying and secrecy, but she loyally wanted the Tans to win.

They were marching up a hill. Cherry noticed that when the column of nurses ahead of her reached the top of the hill, it veered right and entered the shadowy woods. This probably was where they would make camp. When Cherry reached the top of the hill, she looked back. The distant ruby jugs winked at her in the sun, making the location of the Johnson house clear as a map to Cherry. "I must get back there tonight," she thought. "It's only a mile back from here. That isn't too far." She prayed that they wouldn't go too deep into the woods but, come what may, she had to get back to the little injured boy. Her decision made, Cherry cut short her worrying and entered the chill shadowy woods.

In a cleared space, under arching treetops, jeeps, tanks, and trucks were already bustling around. Men in green fatigues hastily and softly unloaded supplies; other men set up gun emplacements; still others gathered for a low-voiced assembly. Cherry went on with her own group deeper into the woods.

Here, in a comparatively protected and camouflaged spot, some more fatigue-clad soldiers were putting up hospital tents. Bunce and the other corpsmen were unpacking medical supplies and instruments, with "Ding" Jackson and Lex directing them. Cherry saw Paul Endicott slowly ride by in his jeep, one of the few men not in fatigues, checking the medical group with his list.

Paul saw Cherry, and he saw Lex. But he made no sign of recognition, preferring to preserve strict military discipline. Cherry's chief concern now, though, was to get that thirty-pound pack and mess kit off her back. She did not dare remove her gas mask, nor her three-pound helmet, nor her pistol belt with its first-aid packet.

The pack off, she stood looking around in amazement at the field hospital which was mushrooming into existence. One heavy tent, shaped like a pyramid, for surgery, was going up at Colonel Wylie's orders. Gwen called her to come pitch their own shelter tent. Suddenly there was a heavy, deafening, pounding roar. The earth shook and Cherry clung wildly to a tree trunk. Ann threw herself flat at Cherry's feet.

"That's our firing batteries at the other end of the bivouac area!" Sergeant Deake shouted over the uproar. "You'd better get used to the sound of a barrage of big guns!"

The pounding of heavy artillery went on, firing blank ammunition over their heads toward the oncoming Blues. The nurses hastily remembered to camouflage their net-covered helmets with leaves and black their faces. "Look out!" Sergeant Deake signaled them. Cherry whirled to see the sergeant tossing practice grenades at them. Surprise drill! The nurses instantly threw themselves flat.

"Never a dull moment," Cherry panted as the puffs of white sulphur smoke cleared away, and the girls gingerly got back on their feet.

The wiry little sergeant called through his hands, "Okay. Nurses. Now set up your tents!"

Pitching pup tents was fun. It did not take long for Cherry and Gwen, working together, to put up theirs. Each girl put up the half of the tiny tent she had carried. "Real homelike," was Gwen's tongue-in-cheek verdict.

"Homelike for a pup," Cherry said, crawling in and promptly backing out again. "Nice in there if you like to suffocate. Come on, I see patients . . . already!"

Although a rough dispensary was just shaping up and the cots barely had been set up under the trees, five soldiers hobbled in for treatment. These "casualties," even before the "action" began, consisted of a sprained ankle, an enormous bee bite, and three upset stomachs. But a little later, Cherry was startled to see Bunce and another corpsman carrying a young man on a litter toward the hospital tents. This soldier was unconscious and badly hurt. Cherry was at his side in an instant.

"He was thrown from a jeep," Bunce blurted out. His young face was anxious and strained, but he reported clearly, "Looks like he's sustained a fracture of the left hip and leg. He had a lot of pain, sir, so I gave him a sedative." Cherry had not seen Lex come up. They looked at each other quickly. "George and I went back half a mile for him when we heard about it. Thought we'd better carry him than drive him . . . not so rough," Bunce finished.

"Good work," Lex commented. "You know a lot for a corpsman." Cherry smiled proudly at her corpsmen. Lex added, "We'd better get to work on that leg."

Before they could start to the hospital tent, Captain Endicott drove up again in his jeep, slowed, and glanced into the litter.

"I'd like a report," he said curtly to Lex.

"First we'll take care of the patient, then you'll get your report," Lex replied, equally curt. He said to Bunce and George, "Take the patient in at once."

"Just a minute, Smith!" Paul Endicott unexpectedly turned on Bunce. "On bivouac, you take your orders from me, not Upham. You'll take that patient in *after* you've given me a report."

Bunce looked uncertain. Cherry sprang forward, anxious for the patient's safety. She knew Bunce was more concerned about that than for the details of military regulations.

"We can't report until we've examined the man!" she tried to put Paul off with tact. "You understand that it's necessary to——"

Lex impatiently brushed her aside. "I'll get Captain Endicott out of the way myself, Nurse!"

"Watch your tongue, Captain Upham!"

There would have been a nasty quarrel if Colonel Wylie had not called out from a tent doorway:

"What's going on out there? Why are you letting that patient wait?"

Instantly the group broke up, and the patient was carried into the tent. In the tent Cherry watched Lex set the leg, quickly and skillfully. Bunce and another corpsman came and carried the patient out to a cot. Bunce would watch him constantly.

Lex was grumbling to himself. Cherry took a deep uncertain breath. Cherry knew, and Lex knew, that Paul Endicott was either waiting outside or would come back soon for the report.

"But, after all, getting the report is Paul's job," Cherry said to Lex.

"That's not what I'm griping about," Lex said. His tawny eyes searched her face. "I'm annoyed with you!"

"Me! What did I do?"

"Why did you have to make excuses to Endicott?" Lex demanded. "Don't you know the patient comes first?"

"Certainly. I was thinking of the patient! But I was also trying to save Bunce from another scrape!"

Lex turned on his heel and strode out.

Cherry leaned against the tent pole, wondering. Why had she and Lex quarreled over this Endicott incident? She felt wretched about quarreling with Lex, and she suspected he felt just as miserable. She noticed that Paul Endicott did not come back for his report. And Bunce wag missing. Paul must have called the boy to headquarters. Cherry did not like that. She lined up on the chow line for supper with a heavy heart.

Supper made Cherry feel better. Food had been cooked in camp and brought here in trucks. Shallow slit trenches, covered with grates, served as stoves to reheat the food. Cherry moved down the line, her leafy helmet slung over her shoulder now, holding out her mess gear to the boys dishing out food, and received a piping hot supper. It tasted marvelous out in the open air. Then they washed their metal mess kits, and Cherry washed her face in cold spring water out of a bucket hung on a tree. The first brilliant stars reminded her it was nearing time to go back to the Johnson farmhouse. But first, she was on duty until bedtime at ten.

She found the evening irritatingly poky. Back at the hospital tents, everyone was overcome with yawns but Cherry. Two boys came in with poison ivy, and a third soldier seemed to be on the verge of appendicitis. But after these emergencies were taken care of, the evening dragged. The firing had died away, even the birds were quiet. Cherry was impatient to finish her duty and go to the Johnson's. She sat in a tent with Ann and Gwen, folding bandages by carefully dimmed lantern light, and tried to stir those two sleepyheads to conversation.

"If you *must* talk," Gwen protested drowsily, "I did hear one thing. It seems the Blues have learned our location . . . from our artillery fire, of course . . . and they've split their troops in two to encircle us."

"Ah-h-h-h," said Ann, rubbing her eyes.

"Well," Cherry demanded briskly, "that means we Tans have to do something to prevent encirclement and getting captured. What do you suppose we'll do?"

But none of the girls were precisely military strate-
gists. After a few wild guesses, Ann leaned back and
frankly closed her eyes. Cherry turned desperately to
Gwen. She wanted to talk about Sally and Jack
Johnson and what she was going to do. Still, she had
better *not* tell the girls she was going . . . that would
make them guilty, too. Anyway, the redhead, though
her eyes were still open, was asleep for all practical
purposes.

Half an hour later, Cherry had to rouse them and
help them stumble across tree roots to the nurses'
shelter tents. Ann dropped into the tent she was sharing
with Vivian. Gwen dumped herself into the little tent,
half indistinguishable from the bushes, farther down.
Fortunately Gwen was sound asleep on her bedroll
when Cherry crawled in beside her to leave her gas mask
behind.

Through the triangular opening of the tent, Cherry
saw a million stars glittering above the treetops. Were
Sally and Jack and Mr. Johnson waiting for her? Cherry
listened to Gwen's soft, regular breathing. She looked
at the luminous radium dial of her wrist watch. Only a
little after ten. She knew she should not leave camp.
None of the nurses knew she was leaving. But she had
promised Sally she would come!

Impulsively, Cherry wiggled out of the tent and
slipped away. She could hardly see the toy-size tents,

scattered and camouflaged as they were, under the dark concealing cover of trees. Tiptoeing away, she gained the sentry's post under a tree some fifty yards ahead. He was a corpsman patrolling the nurses' area.

As she came up, he said, " 'Evening, Lieutenant!"

"Good evening. I want to leave bivouac on urgent business."

"Well, ma'am, an officer doesn't usually need permission to leave, if he or she is going within ten miles and will return in four hours. But it's different on bivouac."

"Oh, I'm not going that far!" Cherry said. Hastily and rather guiltily, she signed the officers' book. She had to get to Sally and Jack. Mr. Johnson probably was anxiously awaiting the nurse, too.

The sentry looked worried. "We're on bivouac, remember. You'd better not go. It might be dangerous."

"What could happen?" she demanded.

"Nothing is certain in the Army but the uncertainty," he warned her.

Cherry hesitated, then thought of the little girl's stricken face. The corpsman sentry watched her doubtfully as she left him. Cherry picked her way through the sleeping camp. Outside the nurses' area, another sentry, posted by H.Q., stopped her again. When Cherry insisted on going on, this sentry hailed the next sentry. Again and again, Cherry was challenged by sentries. Persistently, stubbornly, she argued her way through to the main sentry.

But the main sentry barred her way with his rifle. "You shouldn't go, Lieutenant. The Blues are approaching. They might pick you up and hold you prisoner. Or you might get lost."

Cherry pleaded, "It's an emergency. I'm urgently needed. I'm only going down to that roadside stand. I *couldn't* get lost, that little walk, and if I should, there are soldier lookouts along the road to direct me. Besides, the Blues couldn't be here in the next hour, and," she promised earnestly, "I'll surely be back by then! I wouldn't leave the area if it weren't a real emergency!"

The sentry lowered his rifle, but he said warningly, "I don't know what the Commanding Officer would say if he heard about this. I'm only a private, I can't stop an officer. You're going at your own risk."

Cherry started off doubtful but determined. She carefully noted the two tall pines at the camp's entrance to the woods. Knowing that the children were counting on her, her earlier fatigue seemed to melt away. Cherry hurried along the night road in the frosty country air. The road was quite bright, full of blue moonlight. Here and there a jeep or soldiers in two's passed her. No one stopped her, her nurse's coveralls were her guarantee. If the Blues were really on their way, she certainly could not see or hear them. She memorized landmarks so that she could find her way back—a big oak, a bend in the road, a broken fence. She was worried about leaving bivouac and she was worried lest four-year-old Jack might have suffered seriously from this delay. She must treat him quickly and get right back. The last quarter mile, she ran.

When Cherry knocked on the farmhouse door, Sally opened it. "I knew you'd come!" she cried. Behind her was a tall, worn-looking man in blue jeans, the children's father.

"I sure am glad you came, Nurse," Mr. Johnson said, shaking her hand for a long time. "My wife's in the hospital and I just don't know how to——"

Cherry released her hand and glanced quickly around the farm kitchen. "Well, don't worry," she said. "We'll have Jack fixed up in no time."

But when they led her upstairs into a little dormer room and Cherry saw the limp, towheaded little boy, she knew he could not be "fixed up in no time." He had a nasty cut, and there was danger of infection. Cherry would have to work long and carefully to get the boy out of danger.

She sent Sally downstairs to boil water, and sent Mr. Johnson to sterilize seissors and pliers, in place of any other equipment, and spread the contents of her first-aid kit on a table. Meanwhile, she talked softly and reassuringly to little Jack. It seemed forever until his father and Sally returned with the things Cherry had requested. Then, with their assistance, she set to work. But they were slow and fumbling and upset, and made Cherry's work harder instead of easier. She had to work slowly, too, to spare Jack pain.

With the wound treated and dressed, Cherry realized that her work was only half done. She sat down and explained to Mr. Johnson, and to Sally too, how to take care of Jack and how to change the dressing. "And now," Cherry said, with a distressed look at her wrist watch, "I must be going. It's very late." She had been here all of two hours!

"Thank you, thank you!" Mr. Johnson and Sally cried, as she hurried downstairs and out the door. And the little girl called, "I knew you'd come!"

Cherry smiled and waved. She felt almost as relieved as they did. But . . . *two hours!* She anxiously turned into the road.

She hurried along as fast as she could. It was darker now, for the moon was behind the clouds. She did not meet even one soldier on her way back. That gave her a pang. Was she on the right road? Yes, there was the big oak, and here was the broken fence. She had taken the right turning, all right. But it was curious that the road was so empty. There were no sounds, either, from her own camp nor from the "enemy," only faint night rustlings.

It was a relief to climb the last shadowy incline and see the tall pines that flanked the entrance to camp. This was the spot—those pines were unmistakable!

But where was the sentry?

And where were the rows of tents?

Cherry fearfully peered into the woods. There was not a sign of a living creature, not a tent, not even the most guarded flicker of light, nor a sound in these dense shadows. There was nothing but tree trunks and a black roof of leaves. She must have picked the wrong spot to enter this far-flung wood, she thought, her heart sinking.

She stepped back and surveyed the pines again. No, these were the same two pines. She remembered them clearly, one with its top like a steeple. This road was the right road, too. But how could it be? Where was everyone? She must be dreaming! The camp had vanished!

Cherry shivered. "How could so many men and tons of equipment and heavy field mortars and tanks and jeeps all just . . . just disappear in a puff of smoke? In only two hours? Surely I must be in the wrong spot!"

She ventured a little way into the tangled forest. There she dimly made out tire and tank tracks in the earth, many footprints, and fresh holes where tent stakes had been. This was the place, all right! She was *not* dreaming. The camp had been here and gone!

Trembling all over, Cherry tried to figure out what must have taken place. They had broken camp, in secrecy and haste and silence, and moved on. Why? She remembered the advancing Blues. Her own Tans must have evacuated to avoid being encircled. They had moved to a spot the Blues would not guess. "And a location I can't guess, either," Cherry thought desperately.

She ran to the road and peered in all directions. But she could see little on the night-clouded roads and misty fields. Certainly she could not see, nor hear, any troops moving, whether Tans or Blues.

Suddenly she was terribly frightened. She was lost in the woods, alone, at night!

"Oh, what am I to do?" Cherry gasped. She sank down on a big stone, nearly crying. She never could find her own unit in the dark, in unknown countryside! Maybe the Blues would not come by this way, either, to pick her up. She could not stay alone in the woods all night! Cherry shuddered. She tried hard to think.

She might go back to the Johnson's and ask the family to let her stay overnight. But by now, the road back was deserted and very dark . . . not a safe place to go walking alone. "Besides, I'm a soldier now," Cherry thought. "If I went to the farmhouse, it would be desertion or something really bad like that. Oh, heavens! How foolhardy I was! Those sentries *told* me not to go!"

She got up off the stone and started walking aimlessly around and around in the dark, before the two tall pines. She had not the faintest idea of what to do next. Slight animal noises from the woods, a crackle of a twig, the wind's sudden sigh, stretched her nerves taut. The night was growing colder. She shivered under her coveralls.

Out of the weedy moaning of the wind, she thought she heard a voice. She backed in fright into a dense shadow. Whatever it was, she did not want to face it alone!

The voice went on, calling, calling. Cherry thought of all the dread possibilities that voice might mean and felt her own voice die in her fear-tightened throat. Gradually, as the voice grew nearer, she made out that it called her own name.

Then on a little hillock, silhouetted against the chilly moon, she saw a tall, wild figure, hitching up his trousers with a well-known gesture. Bunce!

She ran forward, voiceless, but waving her arms wildly. Bunce saw her and came running too.

"You crazy idiot!" he yelled at her. They abruptly halted face to face. "Beg your pardon, Lieutenant—gee whiz, I was worried! You all right, Miss Cherry?"

Cherry gasped and found her voice. "Yes . . . I'm . . . all right. What are you doing here?"

"Waited for you, of course!"

"But you shouldn't have. An enlisted man has no right to go off on his own. Bunce, you'll be in trouble."

He took off his jacket and put it around her. *"You're* not in trouble, I s'pose? Why, Miss Cherry, when the girls found out you weren't there and they had to go on without you . . . why, they cried! Miss Jones and Miss Evans and Miss Warren came running and told me. They were scared to report it to anyone else, I guess."

Cherry was slowly gathering her wits together. "Does Captain Upham know? Or Colonel Wylie?" Bunce shook his head. That was a relief! "Does Captain Endicott know?"

The boy managed a laugh, "Gosh, I hope not! 'Specially after that little tussle I had with him this afternoon. Say, where were you, anyhow?"

Cherry confessed.

"Well, it sounds like those kids needed help," Bunce sympathized. "Come on now. I know where they went. We can catch up if we walk fast!"

They started down the road at a fast trot. Suddenly they heard a jeep's motor. Around the bend of the road, the vehicle whirled toward them, and Cherry exclaimed, "Thank goodness! They've sent someone back for us!"

"You think that's good, do you?" Bunce muttered.

The jeep bounced up, throwing dust and pin points of blackout lights on them, and screeched to a sharp stop. Beside the expressionless driver was Captain Endicott. He got out. He was too disgusted for a moment to speak.

"Lieutenant Ames! Are you all right?"

"Yes, sir," Cherry quavered. She added in a whisper, "I went back to those children."

"You broke my specific order, Lieutenant Ames," Captain Endicott said sharply. His handsome face was coldly official. He might never have seen Cherry before. "As for you, Smith," he said with icy dislike, "leaving your post against orders constitutes insubordination. Your motive has nothing to do with breaking discipline. You should have reported Lieutenant Ames's being missing at once, instead of taking matters into your own hands."

Cherry started to defend him, "But Private Smith only meant to——"

Captain Endicott silenced her. "And I'll thank you not to interfere! Now get into that jeep, both of you."

Cherry and Bunce mournfully climbed into the back seat. As the jeep jounced along, they looked at one another but decided against talking. First she had a quarrel with Lex and now she had further antagonized Endicott! And poor Bunce probably was on his way to the guardhouse—on her account!

~~~~~~

CHAPTER VI

Secret Journey

A FEW MORNINGS LATER, CHERRY WAS AT THE GUARD-house on her lunch hour, paying a visit. The guard let Bunce come out into the cheerless corridor. He and Cherry sat down morosely, side by side on a hard wooden bench.

"I guess you know what I came to say," she started, smoothing her olive drab cape. "Thank you and . . . I'm sorry."

Bunce grinned at her. "Aw, don't be sorry, Miss Cherry. I'm used to this place, sort of at home here by now. Besides, didn't you hear about me going hunting?"

Cherry's dark eyes sparkled, but she tried to look disapproving, as Bunce explained. Unable to resist the fall weather, the woods full of animals, and all those rifles around, he had reverted to his happier civilian

110

habits. He had gone AWOL for one glorious day. When he returned with a nice bag, the Commanding Officer sent the game to the kitchens and Bunce to oblivion. Cherry shook her head at him. Going AWOL was bad enough, but obtaining ammunition for personal use was a very serious offense.

"Only one thing I really mind," Bunce finished thoughtfully. "Mom might hear about my bouncing around. She's workin' so hard in a war factory, I'd be kind of sorry to worry her, or anything."

"Then why don't you behave?" Cherry asked, laughing a little. "Honestly, now, *why* don't you behave yourself? You could get promoted to medical technician and go to the Army Medical Technicians' School—that's al-most as good as being a doctor, you know—if you'd only reform."

Bunce shrugged his big, loosely knit shoulders. "I guess I might, if you were around all the time to keep after me. But now that you're goin' away I guess I might as well say good-by to you now forever."

"Why, what in the world do you mean?" Cherry was startled at Bunce's long face.

"Well, you'll be leaving any minute. Shucks, your training's over. And then you'll go somewhere and I'll go somewhere and we'll never see each other any more." He scraped one big foot unhappily along the floor.

"We might meet again some place else," Cherry suggested.

But Bunce dolefully shook his head. "Good-by, Miss Cherry. You've been real nice to me. Well . . . good luck." The guard came and took him back.

Cherry was half-amused, half-shaken by Bunce's sudden and dolorous farewell. But the boy proved to be right. That very afternoon the Chief Nurse called all of Cherry's unit off the wards for an emergency meeting.

"From this moment," she told them, "you and the entire Spencer unit are on alert. You are to hold yourselves in instant readiness for departure at any hour of the day or night. I cannot tell you your destination; for reasons of security, I do not even know myself. You are to go back to your duties, but your bags must be packed, your quarters in perfect order. You will preserve the strictest secrecy, and exercise all your discretion. No one but yourselves is to know you are alerted. All this is for your own safety." And with that, the stern Chief Nurse dismissed them.

The girls did not discuss the great news, even in attention-inviting whispers, until they were safely within the privacy of their own quarters. Then questions and speculations had a field day, as excited girls piled into Cherry's room.

A few things they managed to figure out by common sense. If no one knew exactly when they were leaving, or where they were going, no one could interfere maliciously with their vital travel. Probably, too, the uncertainty of when they were to leave meant they had to go when there happened to be trains and ships free to take them. They got that far, then the meager, stubborn facts yielded no more.

There was more hushed, excited talk that night with "Ding" and Lex and Hal Freeman in one of the medical buildings. The girls were bursting with rosy hopes and romantic notions. Lex told them bluntly:

"It isn't going to be a joy ride. You won't end up in a resort. Better not fool yourselves with a lot of fine ideas, or you'll be awfully disappointed later."

Cherry would have said something, but their quarrel on bivouac still rankled a little. Gwen protested, "Oh, Dr. Lex, you're such a killjoy! Why can't you let us have a little fun?"

"Because it's important to know the truth," Lex said uncompromisingly. "I know you don't like me for it. The truth is seldom popular."

They did not like him for it. However, his words did sober them. They all recognized that Lex usually saw farther and more clearly than the others.

Cherry wondered whether Dr. Joe was going with the unit. Early the next morning, she managed to reach him on the telephone.

"Yes, I know what you want to ask me," Dr. Joe said. "The answer is that I'm permanently attached to the

Spencer unit . . . Yes, I'm glad, too . . . Have you heard
from your mother? . . . Wish I could see Midge, but it's
too far . . . Well, Cherry, I'll see you as soon as I can."
And he hung up. It was an unsatisfactory conversation.
Apparently Dr. Joe could not talk about his work. But
at least she knew, now, that Dr. Joe would go overseas
with Spencer unit. It was not the end of Dr. Joe.

It was the end of Paul Endicott, thank goodness.
Cherry hoped that now, with their leaving, Vivian
would forget him. Vivian was fretting because she could
not say good-by to Endicott. Cherry thought of saying
good-by to Bunce. But that was forbidden. Cherry
tensely went about her ward duties that morning. She
was thinking of home and her family, especially of her
mother. But there was nothing that she, or any of them,
could do except wait from hour to hour, even from
minute to minute. In her room, closet and bureau were
emptied, her bag was packed, the room ready for instant
inspection. At two that afternoon they were called to
stand inspection. But then they were sent back to their
duties, more keyed up than ever. The call might come
at any moment.

Now that she knew she was leaving, Fort Herold
suddenly became dear to Cherry. Walking across the
Post late that same afternoon, she noted for the final
time the sign in the admission hut, "We do the difficult
immediately, the impossible takes a little longer" . . .

heard the cafeteria juke box playing a peppy song, and far off, a band playing a march . . . gazed upon the long, low, wooden barracks with the rays of the setting sun slanting down the neat company streets. A cannon boomed once, a bugle rang out. Retreat! Jeeps and olive drab cars stopped in the roads where they were, near and far soldiers and nurses halted and faced toward the flag, toward the center and heart of the Post. The bugle blew retreat. Cherry, saluting, watched the American flag slowly flutter down. Two soldiers caught it as the bugle's notes rang around the sky and trembled in the fading air. The camp, deeply stirred and with a renewed sense of unity, slowly moved again. The day was over.

Before daybreak the following morning, at five A.M., Cherry was awakened and told that a train was waiting for the Spencer unit. She dressed swiftly, took her suitcase, and with the other girls, rapidly boarded a bus in the chill gray light. Fort Herold did not see them streak down the withering country roads. The train reserved for them carried other troops too, sleepy boys in olive drab who waved at them out the window as the nurses boarded their own car. Cherry was filled with strange feelings. They slipped away like thieves, under cover of darkness and silence. So this was what war was like!

But when the train pulled into the edge of New York City at eight A.M., it certainly was exciting to feel the pulse of the great nervous city, to see its silvery towers glinting in the sun and clouds. And when the girls were promptly treated to breakfast in huge, jammed Pennsylvania Station, Cherry began to enjoy things. After breakfast, pushing through the crowded station, Cherry marveled at the numbers of soldiers and sailors here, going, coming, saying joyous hellos or difficult good-bys to their families and their girls. On a lower level, she saw a hundred boys in olive drab rise from benches, hoist their enormous barracks bags to their backs, and gamely if wistfully start off. Something caught in Cherry's throat, seeing the lonesomeness in their young faces. "I'm glad I'm going to be on hand to take care of them," she thought. Indeed, Cherry and all the girls, judging by their proud, determined faces, planned to win this war all by themselves.

Their next train—were they going north or south or west?—was a great, sleek, transcontinental "flier" with endless chains of Pullmans and dining cars and a lounge car. "We must be going a long way," she realized.

They traveled all day. By twilight Cherry saw that the fields whizzing by outside were softer and still green. They were going south! But how far south? And from there, what corner of the world would they sail to? Cherry was torn between thrills and serious idealism and a sinking sensation in the pit of her stomach. They ate in the dining car that night, where an elderly, imposing Colonel invited Cherry and Ann to share his table, making them feel that the President of the United States himself was counting on them personally. They slept in Pullman berths, to the singing of steel wheels on rails. They rode a second day and a second night.

When Cherry awoke in her berth, the third morning, she missed the rocking sensation she had become used to. The train was standing still. She peeked out from behind the green blind and saw porters wheeling crates of luggage, soldiers standing on a platform smoking, people hurrying to a waiting train.

She tumbled out of her berth and woke the other nurses.

"We're here!" she announced excitedly, brushing her black curls out of her eyes. "Get up! We're here!"

"We're where?" practical Bertha Larsen wanted to know.

"I don't know where, but we're here!" Cherry wiggled into her clothes, ran into the tiny washroom, gave her face and teeth a lick and a promise, and raced out onto the station platform. The other nurses quickly followed her, and they all climbed into special busses. Riding, she saw something so beautiful and so telltale that she gasped.

There, tossing and sparkling in the southern sun, lay a tropical blue sea, seemingly strewn with diamonds.

"What is that body of water?" she asked the soldier bus driver. The man said in a soft Southern drawl, "Why, chile, that's the Gulf of Mexico! Ain't she pretty?"

"She certainly is," said Gwen from the seat ahead.

"Beautiful!" exclaimed Ann beside her. "The Gulf of Mexico can take us a lot of places," she said thoughtfully. "South America, Mexico or into the Pacific via the Panama Canal."

"If you know so much geography," Cherry teased, "what town are we in?"

They found out later, after they had been comfortably installed in a big hotel and rigidly signed in. The hotel had been taken over by the Army. This southern city, where they exchanged near-winter for summer, dripped with lacy black iron balconies, flowering palm trees, and hospitality. The most hospitable of all was the Nurse Major, to whose administrative office near the docks they were promptly taken.

Major Dorothy Deane was lively and pretty and sympathetic. This pert lady, who made them all comfortable the moment they came in and who did *not* sit behind her big desk, had served with the Army in France in 1918, had worked in South America, in the Philippines, in the Orient. Now, she said with a laugh, she was "chained to that desk" while her several thousand charges did the traveling.

Then she proceeded to give them full instructions to govern their activities while in the port city. "You must be in rooms at 11:00 P.M., unless given a pass . . . *no long distance calls* . . . no *telegrams* or *postcards* are to be used in communicating with friends or families . . . you must not hint to *anyone* that you are leaving the port."

The nurses looked at her expectantly, wondering if they were going to learn their destination.

Major Deane smiled. "No, I am not the itinerary department. All I can tell you is that a certain general asked me for a certain number of nurses in a certain place at a certain time. Now that you know your destination," the girls' laughter interrupted her, "you can complain to me about training or equipment or the clothes you wear. I help plan 'em. And please do speak up, if you want to gripe or ask questions or advice. That's what I'm here for."

After some informal talk back and forth with the girls, Major Deane grinned and said, "That's fine. I hope you'll write to me from overseas, or drop into my office whenever you're in town again. You'd be proud of some of the letters I get from our Army nurses. Those girls are brave, and how they use their heads!"

She told them about an emergency in North Africa, when the wounded were brought in before a hospital was set up for them. "On top of that, the supplies had been sunk, there weren't even bandages," Major Deane told them. "So our nurses tore up G.I. underwear and *made* bandages! Incidentally, you'd better buy plenty of underwear and stockings to take along. I'll give you a list of recommended purchases, and you can shop within the next few days. You're going to find," she warned them laughingly, "that the natives will want your lieutenant's bars for souvenirs, and you'll discover yourself in mud up to your knees sometimes, or facing a real emergency of no bobby pins and no cold cream! So off with you! Get processed and go shopping!

She shooed them out, with instructions to come back tomorrow. In the meantime, they had this whole golden, summery day before them, and a million things to do. First came "processing."

This complicated and somewhat tedious business took place in what Cherry learned was called a staging area. It was dramatically near the docks and the sea. Led by a Chief Nurse, they marched around from Army Nurse Corps buildings to Army depots to Army sheds, having things done to them. They were given "shots" to immunize them against yellow fever. Then they were blood typed, a process familiar to these nurses. Then Cherry and her friends received their metal identification tags. Cherry's tag bore her name, rank, serial number and blood type, nearest relative

and address, religion, tetanus inoculation date. The
few who had not already done so at Herold before their
training began, now took out Army insurance. They
received their pay; they would receive twenty per cent
more than base pay as soon as they were overseas.

Cherry decided to sign an allotment sending home
half of her future pay to her mother. There'd be little
to spend it on, wherever she was going. Cherry also
arranged to have some of her pay deducted and invested
in War Bonds for herself.

Getting their field equipment was lots of fun. The
girls received an olive drab herringbone work suit,
consisting of blouse, well cut trousers, high field shoes,
leggings, and helmet. They looked at these garments
dubiously.

"It's funny about this particular uniform," the Chief
Nurse said, laughing. "Nurses are about the best
dressed group in uniform, but this work suit . . . well!
One of the enlisted men in Sicily came into the Army
doctor's tent and asked to have his eyes examined. He
said 'I see a lot of soldiers coming up the road, but they
all have girls' heads!'"

The girls laughed and felt refreshed. They were
getting tired, but not too tired to be excited over the field
equipment issued them. A mute promise of adventure
was issued along with the bedroll, mattress covers, blan-
ket, tent, tent poles and pins. "You won't have to carry

this," the Chief Nurse told them. "It will be packed for you and the corpsmen will put up your tents for you." Next came a tropical cork-lined helmet, which set Cherry to guessing, field bag, first-aid kit, more and more things. They also received, for overseas ward duty, a brown and white seersucker dress with a matching jacket for street wear. Her eyes began to feel heavy as the processing went on.

Cherry was glad to get back to the hotel that warm, southern evening. She even treated herself to a nap before dinner. Processing was quite a process! But after a pleasant dinner, she perked up when Vivian suggested that they all go sightseeing.

"I have an idea," Cherry said.

"You always have ideas," Josie Franklin said enviously.

"Not always such good ones, either," Ann put in. "For instance——"

"Quiet! This idea is guaranteed harmless." Cherry thought it would be fun to hire two or three of the old-fashioned, horse-drawn hansoms she had seen on the cobblestoned streets. Eight of them hired cabs, and drove leisurely down moonlit streets under giant moss-hung trees, breathing in freesia and tuberose. There were red poinsettias growing everywhere, looking oddly Christmasy in this land of summer. Much as Cherry loved this lush, languorous place, she was impatient to finish with waiting . . . restless to plunge ahead to her final destination.

In the following days, they saw delightful Major Deane again, filled out papers, addressed safe arrival cards which would later be forwarded to their families, and best of all went shopping. Cherry already had bought a foot locker, which served as a small trunk but could stand unobtrusively at the foot of a bed or cot. Now she shopped for all kinds of everyday personal supplies, like needles and thread, sunburn lotion, and flashlight batteries. She was fortunate enough to find a tiny portable radio, which she purchased on sight.

Besides their strange assortment of necessary articles, the nurses bought souvenirs for cheering up their unknown patients, candy for the children who were sure to be about, and had a final fling at the beauty shops. The girls were comparatively free after official business to go sight-seeing or to the theater, but actually this waiting was tedious. Cherry grew more and more restless. She packed her white uniforms in her bedding roll, put the heavier garments in the foot locker, stowed just enough things for the voyage in her small suitcase, and waited. Why didn't they get started? Where was their ship? But another day, and still another day, slipped by.

Cherry had a great deal of time to think. She wondered where Lex was. She had known all along, of course, that Captains "Ding" Jackson, and Hal Freeman, and Colonel Wylie himself, had arrived with them and were sailing with them. It was strange that there was no word of Lex and of Dr. Joe. Inquiries, she knew, were useless.

Most of all, Cherry thought poignantly of her family in Hilton, and of the inspired adventure which was taking her farther and farther away from them. She reread their last letters, and longed to see them again. Yet she was leaving them so that she might have a free family and a safe home town to return to. She hoped with all her heart that she would measure up to the unknown responsibilities she had sworn to undertake. Many lives hung in the balance. Searchingly, Cherry asked herself, "Am I not too young? Too inexperienced?" But many other Army nurses were as young and green as she, yet they were doing a magnificent job all over the world. "I hope I'm as good as they are, as brave and skillful. If only I could be sure . . ." But there was no way to know except to test herself against the steely reality. And that most serious of all tests still lay ahead.

Then one night they were roused out of their sleep, told in whispers the moment had come. They dressed swiftly and silently, snatched up their suitcases, left the hotel, and were gone in the night.

At the dock, in the dark and the tense silence, Cherry and her fellow nurses lined up beside, almost beneath, the swelling steel hulk of the great ship. She heard the lapping of water, hurried footsteps, terse commands, the low purr of engines. The girls were in uniform, with gas mask, helmet, and canvas bag slung from their shoulders. They stood in silence. Colonel Wylie and Major Dorothy Deane and an unknown officer came by with flashlights. Then the officer quietly called off their names one by one "Aarons . . . Ackland . . . Allen . . . Ames . . ."

Cherry responded by reciting her serial number. The flashlights flared briefly on her face, and she groped her way up the gangplank to the huge blacked-out transport. She was aboard!

Cherry made out a milling but orderly crowd of soldiers on the black decks of the troopship. In the half dark, she saw Captain "Ding" Jackson and Captain Freeman. Like everyone else, she leaned over the rail, trying to see what was going on below. At one end of the ship, under a small shielded light, supplies were being loaded. "Hope it's candy," she heard one soldier say.

"Boy, what this boy wouldn't give for a chocolate bar right now!" came another voice with an unmistakable Middle West twang. "Or some good old rabbit stew out of those rabbits I shot myself!"

The first voice, amazed, said, "Were you allowed . . ."

"Did the C.O. give you leave to go hunting?" Cherry began to listen with some attention.

"Why, sure!" The owner of the blithe voice straightened up from the ship's rail and his tousled head towered against the steam-clouded night sky. "The C.O. said to me, 'Doc, you've been working too hard. You're a mighty valuable man. Why don't you take the day off and——'"

"Bunce!" Cherry stopped him. It was part protest, part greeting.

"Land's sakes! Miss Cherry! And hot on my trail!"

Cherry and her irrepressible corpsman practically fell into each other's arms. She barely noticed that cranes were lifting the gangplanks away, the engines throbbed louder, and the whole ship started to vibrate and slip away.

"Bunce," Cherry shouted joyfully over the engine noise and fumbled in her bag, "here's three chocolate bars for you and your hungry friends! And what's more, now that I've found you again, you certainly are going to behave!"

~~~~~~

CHAPTER VII

Señorita Cherry

BLUE SKIES, BLUE WATER, YOUNG FACES ON THE SUNNY decks . . . and now, on the watery horizon, rose a purple silhouette of land. Cherry leaned against the ship's rail, along with the crowds of soldiers, and stared. As their ship plowed nearer, she excitedly made out beaches fringed with palm trees, and blue mountains rising sheerly out of the sand.

Cherry took a deep breath of the sweet, hot, ripe wind from land. "It even smells exotic," she thought. She could almost imagine strange music, fiery mountains, and voices clattering in a new tongue. "But where are we?"

A metallic voice presently rumbled out of the ship's loud-speaker. "We are approaching the Republic of Panama. We stop briefly at the port of Cristobal, then continue via the Panama Canal to Panama City."

127

"The announcer makes it sound so prosaic," Cherry mourned to "Ding" Jackson, who had pushed through the crowd to her side.

The lanky New Englander grinned. "Why, girl, Central America is one of the most romantic little stretches of land in the world! Look here!" On the back of a prescription pad, he drew Cherry a tiny map. It showed a long, very thin, crooked piece of land, like a turkey's neck. These few little miles of land were all that connected the vast northern and southern continents of the two Americas, all that separated the mighty Atlantic from the endless Pacific. "But the oceans aren't separated any longer," "Ding" said. "The Panama Canal, which the United States built and operates through treaty and purchase from Panama, cuts right through."

Their boat nosed its way into Cristobal. Cherry saw, lying in its harbor, warships and merchant ships flying the flags of Russia, China, England, Canada, South Africa! Panama was certainly an international zone! The Cristobal docks rang with staccato words of Spanish, flashed with dark Latin and Indian and Negro faces. Cherry nearly fell over the rail watching the longshoremen on the pier below. They were loading huge boxes and bales onto ships bound for the States.

"Pirate treasure," "Ding" nudged her. "Pirates used to hide in Panama and waylay ships bringing jewels from the Orient, or caravans laden with gold from Brazil.

In Panama City, which they burned and sacked, you might still find a stray ruby stolen from India, buried deep in the sand!"

On the dock below, something else caught Cherry's attention. Several brisk young men, Americans, were giving the ship opposite Cherry's own a thorough, rapid search. They were the G-men of health safety . . . on the trail of germs, fever-bearing mosquitoes, and disease. They worked relentlessly with the military in charge of the Panama Canal Zone. Cherry knew that these men of the United States Public Health Service were as adventurous and daring, fighting disease in the Rockies, in the Louisiana swamps, or here in ocean-bound Panama, as any pirates had ever been. No ship, plane, train or auto could move across an American border until these men were satisfied that no infection was being carried from one land to another. And no wonder, for an epidemic can kill more thousands than bombs.

Out of Cristobal, the most amazing part of their journey began. It was fascinating to float down the intricate man-made canals and locks, to look from deck to land. Panama was a land of volcanos, of hilly tawny earth, of steamy jungle, and flowering plantations. Everything was lush, tropical, intensely colored under the densely purple sky and the fierce burning rays of the sun.

That night, Cherry looking from deck at the passing beautiful hilly country, lying so still and peaceful under the brilliant star-studded sky, wondered what adventure lay before her in this picturesque land.

Next morning, in Panama City, the girls disembarked and clambered onto busses. Cherry was eager to go sightseeing, but they were urgently needed at the Army base hospital. So she had to satisfy herself with glimpses from the bus of Latin-American Panama City, and its sister American city, Ancon, where they were to live and work.

Everywhere were white stone government buildings in Roman style, cathedrals of white marble, sunny plazas and pigeons and wide low marble steps. They drove past gardens, behind wrought-iron fences, full of playing fountains and leafy shadow and cabbage-size white and red roses, blooming in this first week in November. Beyond all this, beyond an old fort high on the harbor's hill, lay the Pacific Ocean.

The nurses were led into an exposition building converted to nurses' quarters. "Did you ever see anything so romantic?" Cherry marveled, as they unpacked in a dormitory room. There were eight girls to a smallish room containing double-decker beds.

"Yoo-hoo, I'm Carmen!" Gwen waltzed past her, snapping her fingers, her comb between her teeth. Hi, Señorita Cherry!

"I'm only an imitation!" Cherry took a good-natured poke at her. She slipped into her brown and white seersucker dress, with its matching jacket and jaunty cap. They all went out together in search of a bus.

The girls promptly got lost, wandering through a little park. A frantic Chief Nurse caught up with them.

"A fine way to behave!" she scolded them. She was a lithe and lively woman of about forty, very professional, with reddish brown hair and snapping brown eyes. "What do you girls mean by running out on me? I was delayed at the dock—didn't you get word? I'm Captain Johnny Mae Cowan, your Chief Nurse, and after this you stick close to me!" When they begged for lunch, she had to grin. "Serves you right," she said. "There's a Nurses' Mess waiting for you. And a special bus will take you from quarters to the hospital and back."

Cherry soon saw how badly they were needed. This base hospital had two thousand beds. But instead of the hundred and eighty nurses needed, they had less than a hundred native nurses because the hospital unit assigned there had been reassigned to move on. Fortunately, less than half the beds were full at the moment. But Captain Johnny Mae Cowan warned them, "In the Army, you never know what's coming!" She led them through the wards and Cherry saw another difficulty. This sprawling old building had been enlarged by tacking on wings here and there, so that a single ward stretched out for two or three blocks. One lone nurse responsible for two or three wards would have to run to make her rounds! And if, in an emergency, the cases doubled or tripled overnight . . . !

It was the patients in those beds, however, who concerned Cherry most. These men who lay under khaki blankets, pale under their fading sunburns—some of them were mere boys—smiled when the girls came in. Some of them had been lying there a long time, Captain Johnny Mae Cowan whispered. Some of them had been injured in the line of duty. Some were victims of common illnesses. Cherry saw many post-operative cases, as well. Corpsmen, too, smiled at the new nurses. So did the few native nurses, little dark-eyed girls in white.

From floor to floor, from one sprawling old wing to another, Cherry saw each soldier's face turn on the pillow and light up gratefully as the new nurses came in. "Lord knows they need you!" Johnny Mae Cowan whispered. The girls nodded soberly, but inside, Cherry glowed. One boy weakly called out to her, "Hi, Red Cheeks, it makes me feel better just to look at you!"

When Cherry left the hospital late that afternoon, she did not at first recognize the tall elegant uniformed figure blocking the big door. Then her heart sank, Paul Endicott!

"Hello, Lieutenant Ames. So nice to see you," he said wryly.

"How are you, Captain Endicott? It's a surprise to find you here."

"I'm working with the supply ships leaving this port. I'm also," he added, "still doing liaison work with Spencer unit."

"How nice," Cherry said faintly.

"Is Vivian Warren coming out soon?" Paul asked. He made no further pretense of being friendly with Cherry.

"Yes, Vivian will be right down. See you again." And Cherry left. So she thought she was safely rid of him! She should have known anything can happen in the Army . . . should have guessed that Paul would continue in the same work at home or abroad! She wondered what sort of work he was doing with the incoming and outgoing ships.

Except for the disturbing thought of Endicott, Cherry spent a happy evening with Ann and Gwen. They wandered a while through picturesque markets, then dined by candlelight in an open patio. Later they walked along the crumbling Paseo, arm in arm, in the tropic night.

Cherry was curled up in bed, and the other girls were drifting off to sleep, when Vivian tiptoed into their room. Cherry knew she had had a date with Paul Endicott. Vivian softly came over to Cherry's bed. Cherry grinned at her in the half-light.

"I'm awake. Hello."

Vivian whispered, "There's the most beautiful moon. It really is worth getting up to see."

Cherry understood Vivian was thrilled after her romantic evening, and wanted to tell her about it. She rose, put on her robe and slippers, and the two girls slipped out to a little balcony. The enormous moon shone down with pure blue-white radiance on the sleeping white city.

"Did you ever see such a lovely night," Vivian murmured. Her wistful face, pale in the moonlight, was deeply moved. "Just look at that moon!"

She did not mention Paul. But Cherry knew that it was not the beauty of the night, only a rather shabby sort of man, that stirred Vivian so much. It made Cherry feel terribly sad. Vivian's first taste of happiness might be pathetically short-lived. She should have warned her sooner about Paul. Vivian's danger was growing, she had certainly better not delay that warning any longer. The look on Vivian's dreaming face did not make her task any easier. Cherry chose her words with care.

"Moonlight and romance *are* wonderful, aren't they? It's pretty hard to keep one's head sometimes."

Vivian smiled and admitted, "It is hard to keep your head. But Paul's so sweet to me. Honestly, he's so wonderful, Cherry! Why, this is the nicest thing that's ever happened to me!"

"It must be extra hard," Cherry agreed sympathetically, "to keep your head about Paul Endicott. He really is awfully handsome and charming. I don't want to interfere, Vivian, but . . . anyhow, why don't you think about it a little bit."

The two girls leaned against the balcony rail, drinking in the lovely night and musing. Finally Vivian said earnestly:

"Tell me something, Cherry. I can see you're really worried about me. *Why* don't you like Paul?"

"It's not that I dislike him. I don't. And for all I know, I may be judging him unfairly. Maybe he's every bit as nice as you say he is," Cherry said, bending over backwards to be fair. "But I'm certain of one thing. He is self-centered and I'm just afraid he'll do something to make you unhappy."

"Oh, no!" Vivian protested. "He's too fine! Besides, what could Paul do to hurt me?"

Cherry looked out over the silvery roofs, then back to Vivian. She laughed a little ruefully. It was so hard to make Vivian see. "You've had so many disappointments,

Vivian, I . . . I just hope you don't have another one on Endicott's account."

Vivian sighed. "But it's so *nice*, falling in love . . ." She gave Cherry's arm an affectionate squeeze. "How's about you?"

Cherry grinned and yawned. "If you mean Lex, I don't even know where Lex is. Come on in. What you and I need just now is sleep! In . . . large . . . quantities!" Cherry yawned.

Yet Cherry missed Lex that first week. She had had no word of or from him. Finally one day his familiar voice came over the crackling wire of the ward phone. He sounded warm and reassuring.

"I'm going to work on your ward," he told her. "In about a week!"

"Oh, Lex! I'm so glad!" she replied, and meant it. She waited for the good sight of his solid, reliable figure striding down the ward.

Toward the middle of the month, Cherry looked up from making a bed to see Lex marching down the aisle of beds. With his broad shoulders and competent air, he clearly promised help to these patients. His golden brown eyes sought her out immediately. Cherry was surprised at how glad and relieved she felt to see him.

"It's been a long time," he said to her. Then he looked around the ward. "There's a lot to do here, isn't there? We'll talk tonight, if you can come out." Lex went from bed to bed. He examined, discussed, prescribed, leaving a feeling of security and encouragement among the men.

Cherry met Lex that evening at the Army Hospital's library. When every other doctor and officer despaired of even time to sleep, Lex managed to squeeze in studies of new developments in medicine. As he put aside the pamphlets he was studying, Cherry saw he had something white and lacy in his hand.

"A mantilla for you," he said, and handed it to her.

Cherry thanked him as Lex hurried her out into the cobblestoned street and helped her into an old-fashioned, horse-drawn hansom.

They rode, in the twilight, into the hills. They came to a ranch with a big farmhouse. On its wide porch, under the amber light of lanterns, tables were set. Cherry and Lex chose a corner one which looked far out over the night-shrouded mountains, down into the lighted city, beyond the harbor fortress to the Pacific.

"What a spot!" Cherry murmured, her black eyes widening. She looked back to Lex appreciatively. "I'll bet even that ladies' man Endicott hasn't discovered this place. You know, Lex, he doesn't like me because he suspects I disapprove of him. And because Vivian is one of my best friends, Paul is afraid I'll influence her."

"Quite possible," Lex agreed. "But let's not let him spoil our dinner. What shall we order?"

As they ate, Lex explained why he and Major Fortune had not sailed with the rest of Spencer unit. Dr. Joe had precious drugs and equipment, too precious to risk to enemy submarines. He and Lex had flown to Panama. Since their arrival, they had been secretly—almost under guard—setting up Dr. Joe's laboratory for the field experiment he wanted so urgently to test out. Until now, Lex had been unable to see her. And even now, he hinted at some vague, strange risk.

"Why all the secrecy? What's the danger?" Cherry puzzled. She added wistfully, "I miss seeing Dr. Joe."

Lex filled Cherry's demitasse, then his own, before he replied. "I think," he said slowly, considering his words, "that I'm going to take you to see Dr. Joe. He needs encouragement. It would do him good to see you."

They went on to talk of many other things. Cherry looked at his strong, familiar face smiling at her across the table. It was so satisfying to be with Lex! Lex had asked her an important question just before her graduation and, one of these days, Cherry foresaw, Lex would ask her again, and she did not know what she should reply. It would be only a matter of time. And in the Army, time could be startlingly telescoped.

They left the hacienda in the hills, and when they came back into Panama City, something else roused Cherry's curiosity. Their cab driver, an old man, returned via the native barrio. These narrow, twisting streets were crowded close with square white clay houses, pressing against the sidewalk and each other. But the driver circled his horse past a deserted lane which had no houses, except one at the end which he carefully avoided.

Lex shouted to the driver, "Why are you taking us the long way around?"

The old man turned around. "That house." He pointed. Unlike the others, this dark, empty house stood alone in a wilderness of neglected garden. "That house no good! Don't go near!"

Lex shrugged. "He's superstitious, probably. Well, every town has its haunted house."

The driver turned around again and said insistently, "Not a story. Bad house! Haunted!"

"Did you hear that, Lex?" she said under her breath.

Lex laughed at her. "Oh, pooh! If you want local color, just tie that mantilla over your head!"

Cherry had quite another sort of mystery to think about when Lex took her to visit Major Fortune some afternoons later. Lex was waiting for her when she went off duty. They walked over to a small, guarded laboratory building, in the U.S. Medical Corps area. Entering Dr. Joe's littered research room, they walked into the middle of an argument. Both Major Fortune and Colonel Wylie, Spencer unit's director, were furiously excited.

"I said no and no it remains!" Colonel Wylie was shouting. His steely gray eyes and hawk face made Cherry shudder, not entirely from force of habit. The eminent surgeon was thoroughly, stubbornly angry. "Let me remind you, Fortune, that you as a researcher are present here . . . that you are accompanying this unit . . . solely through my courtesy! You know this isn't a usual arrangement. You simply haven't the time to do research on *two* things. Stick to the one that's militarily necessary, and drop the tropical research! The U.S. Public Health Service is handling that. Your precious time must be used for the other problem. Concentrate on that!"

Dr. Joe started to speak, but Colonel Wylie turned away, refusing to hear another word. Cherry and Lex were standing still in the doorway. Colonel Wylie saw them now, and nodded curtly. Major Fortune came over to Cherry.

"I'm glad to see you, my dear." He put his hand heavily on her shoulder. "I wish I could ask you how Midge and the Ames's and Hilton are."

"Don't worry. They're all right." Cherry smiled her very warmest at him.

Dr. Joe's troubled face cleared a little. He patted her shoulder, and turned away to talk with Colonel Wylie again in low tones. Meanwhile Lex explained to Cherry what all the excitement was about. Dr. Joe wanted to try out new control measures against malaria and similar tropical fevers to protect soldiers from disease in jungle warfare. Lex went on to talk of an extraordinary military base here in Panama. It was a U.S. Army base, but it was carved out of the jungle. No woman had ever been there, and the only men there were our soldiers and Indians.

"Indians?" Cherry echoed.

"Yes, our soldiers in that jungle base owe their lives from day to day," Lex told Cherry, with a warmly appreciative look in his eyes, "to the natives and Indians who work with them. Those Indians know the secrets of the jungle. They know how to fight the jungle. They're fighting this war, too." He continued, "Our soldiers are hard pressed to keep alive in the jungle with its treacherous swamps, its poisonous undergrowth, its dense wildernesses, its deadly creatures—that's where the Indians help—and with its intense wet heat, mosquitoes and the steady threat of malaria—that's where the U.S. Public Health Service comes in, waging a never-relenting war against all carriers and sources of tropical fevers."

Colonel Wylie, who had been listening to Lex, suddenly burst out:

"Exactly. The U.S. Public Health Service is on the job twenty-four hours a day. That's what I've been trying to tell you, Fortune."

Then, seizing his hat, Colonel Wylie strode out.

Cherry saw Dr. Joe's head droop. The straight lock of gray hair fell over one eye. He looked like a disheartened little boy. Cherry felt very sorry for him. She understood how much this new malaria serum meant to Dr. Joe. He, with Lex's assistance, had started research on it back at Spencer . . . had already put in many months on it . . . and here he was in Panama, where an epidemic was a constant threat, with no time for proving his serum. Her heart went out to him and she wanted very much to help her old friend.

Lex and Cherry stayed a while, chatting with Dr. Joe. But the elderly man was upset and preoccupied. He clearly wanted to be left alone. Cherry said good-by to him, and a few minutes later to Lex.

She walked along, unaware of her surroundings, lost in deep thought about poor Dr. Joe and the recent scene she had witnessed. Suddenly she realized that she was in front of the hospital library. She decided to do a little reading on malaria. But the library was just closing.

Cherry worked hard on the wards all this summery month of November. She was assigned to Medical, a long spread-out, old-fashioned three rooms, along with a Panamanian nurse. Rita Martinez was a tiny, wiry, dark little girl, as lively as a sparrow. She had sharp, small features, olive skin, tilted black eyes that gleamed with fun, and a quick smile that showed off perfect white teeth. Her raven black straight hair was knotted demurely under her nurse's cap. As a citizen of an Allied nation, she too was a lieutenant in the Army Nurse Corps, and very proud of it. Rita turned out to be a delight to work with, and Cherry's good friend.

Despite Cherry's being very busy, thoughts of Dr. Joe and the scene in the laboratory occasionally crossed her mind. She had had lectures on malaria in basic, but they were necessarily sketchy lessons. One day, Cherry asked Rita what she knew about tropical fevers. Rita knew a great deal about them. She described the symptoms of such fevers to Cherry. Although the U.S. Public Health Service had it pretty well under control in Panama, there was still tropical fever in the backwoods. Tropical fevers were deadly diseases and Rita hoped some day to specialize in them. Cherry became so interested that she borrowed a reference volume on tropical fevers with the hope that she could somehow find the time to learn more about them.

One of Cherry's ward duties was to train several corpsmen. They, not the nurses, did the actual bedside nursing, and all the handling and lifting of patients, while the nurses supervised. Bunce and George and another boy had been Cherry's corpsmen at Herold, the other six were new. They had had some theory but too little practice. Bunce stood out easily as the best corpsman of the group. He watched the patients as constantly and closely as Cherry herself. He was eager to help and entirely unselfish. But Cherry noted, from his preoccupied grin, and from his whispering with the corpsmen and patients, that Bunce was preparing some deviltry again.

"Don't forget I've got an official eye on you!" Cherry warned him.

"Yes'm," Bunce agreed, his blue eyes twinkling. "If you can reform me, you're good! But if you could," he added almost pleadingly, "before I get into real serious trouble, I'd be much obliged to you!"

He was promoting non-existent stamps among the patients and corpsmen with an ardent sales talk that almost convinced Cherry herself to invest in them. Cherry squelched that quickly.

Rita Martinez had an unquenchable love of mischief, too, Cherry discovered. One day Cherry asked Rita where she had learned to speak such good "American." Cherry was helping her put away linens, for tiny Rita could not reach the top shelves.

"I lived with my aunt in New York. I'll tell you what, Señorita Cherry!" Cherry groaned—what with her black eyes and red cheeks, that nickname was catching on. "I'll teach you to speak Spanish!"

Bunce ambled up just then. He was almost twice as tall as little Rita. The two of them grinned at each other.

"Learn Spanish?" Bunce looked interested too. "Go right ahead—don't mind me."

"All right," Rita said. She primly folded her little hands in front of her apron. "*Loco,* that means Chief Nurse. You call her that. When someone tells you to hurry, you say, "*Si, mañana.* If you want to say——"

"Hey! Just a minute!" Bunce hitched up his trousers in perplexity. "I learned some Spanish in school. *Loco* means crazy—she can't call the Chief Nurse crazy to her face! And if someone says, Hurry, she dasn't say, Yes, *tomorrow.* Say, what is this?"

Rita leaned against the linen closet door, doubled up with laughter. "Why did you have to tell her?"

Bunce's eye kindled, as he joyously if warily recognized a kindred spirit. Cherry was convulsed, too, in spite of her visions of the wild results of Rita's coaching.

"Just wait!" Rita said, still giggling. "I'm going to teach *someone* Spanish yet!"

"Seriously," Cherry pleaded, "teach me a few useful words, like hospital, doctor, nurse, medicine, and . . . uh . . . hello, okay . . . and food! Roast beef, steak, and potatoes."

"Certainly," Rita said. As Cherry and Bunce listened, she reeled off, "El hospital, el doctor, la nurse, el medecino, hóla, okay, rosbif, biftec, patatas." Then she broke down again with laughter.

Cherry and Bunce were reeling. "You're . . . you're kidding us!" Cherry gasped. They choked back their laughter, stopped fooling and got to work.

There was plenty of work on the ward. Cherry was trying to get Medical Ward in top-notch running order. The Chief Nurse and the Ward Officer both had too many duties to give them much help. That, plus the nurse shortage, kept Cherry and Rita busy. Ann and Gwen, who were assigned to the special departments of Receiving and Out-Patient, told Cherry they too wished urgently for more nurses. Cherry worked rather desperately against the day when Colonel Wylie, and probably Liaison Officer Endicott, too, would inspect her ward.

Cherry did not find the going easy. She was on duty seven to eight hours a day, with a half day off each week. On her half day off, she was too tired to wander about Panama City, curious as she was to see it. She merely went back to Nurses' Quarters, dug her way through the double-decker beds and the welter of suitcases, foot lockers, curling irons, drying stockings, cosmetics, snapshots, pausing just long enough to pick up her book on tropical fevers, threw herself on her bunk and started thumbing through the book, picking out sentences here and there. "Yellow fever and malaria are infective tropical fevers, transmitted by the bite of a tropical mosquito. There is danger of epidemic . . .

Malaria causes a higher sick and death rate than any other disease. Preventive inoculations . . . curative serum . . . spray oil to destroy mosquito and larvae." Inoculations . . . oil spray . . . Dr. Joe had devised new and improved versions of those! And his serum was a brand-new type of serum!

Cherry continued to read with more concentrated interest. "Symptoms of malarial fevers are (1st stage) chilliness, shivering, face pale or livid, fingers white . . . (2nd stage) dry heat, skin burning and flushed . . . (3rd stage) profuse sweating.

"Incubation period is four to five days . . . breed in any still water where they can lay eggs . . . telltale film in water. Object . . . to kill larvae before they develop. Guard and treat water supply.

"Rigid quarantine restrictions on infected people. Malaria and related fevers *not* a remote threat. In southeastern U.S., three to five million cases yearly. Spraying and rigid inspection of all planes, ships, trains, autos, before leaving danger area." Cherry thought of the ships of many nations lying in Panama's harbors and shuddered at the thought of a possible epidemic. She read on ". . . *several special forms of malaria* are stamped out in developed countries. But these fevers are still present in South and Central America. They *can come back* to other countries easily." Cherry shuddered again at the horrid thought of what an epidemic would be like, especially now, with a war going on—a war that must be waged with the fewest possible interruptions. Then one sentence seemed to rise off the page in burning letters——

"Severe rare form of malaria called blackwater fever must be treated with serum."

She lay still for a while thinking about Dr. Joe and wishing that he could have had the time to continue with his malaria research and prove his serum. Then she fell fast asleep.

Cherry kept busy on the ward. She longed for her full day off and she hoped that the rest of the month would go by quickly.

"I want *out*—a change, some excitement," she confided to Rita. "I know what I'm going to do. I'm going to explore the haunted house."

Rita said quickly, "The house at the end of the lane?"

"Yes! How did you know?"

Rita frowned a little at the dressing cart she was preparing. "Have you the other scissors? Did you sterilize it?"

"Yes and yes," Cherry said impatiently. "What about that house?"

"Oh, nothing." As Cherry waited, Rita added, "Some silly people say there's a ghost in there."

"You'll have a ghost," Bunce said, suddenly filling the doorway, "if you don't give Williams something to eat! He must be getting well, he claims he's starving again!"

Rita rushed off to her patient. Bunce shuffled into the utility room and perched his lanky length on a white stool beside Cherry. "Mind if I take a break, boss? I've been runnin' my legs off all day."

"Certainly, sit down and rest, Bunce." Cherry went on preparing the dressing cart, while Bunce obligingly handed her things.

"Talkin' about the haunted house, weren't you?" Cherry's big dark eyes flew open in surprise. Bunce grinned. "Oh, I get around. I know that old house. Nobody wants to live in it. Don't know why. Guess it's harmless enough . . . unless there's some ghosts rooming there." Bunce chuckled.

"Well, I'm going to see it on my first free day," Cherry decided aloud. "And if I don't find at least one ghost, I'm going to be darn disappointed. That is, *if* my free day ever, *ever* comes!"

This month of work, though hard, was inspired because of Cherry's soldier patients. Little by little, she was coming to know them . . . the boy who was as much homesick and frightened as physically ill . . . the middle-aged man who knew he was dying of cancer and begged to be allowed to die fighting, rather than go home . . . the boy from a backwoods Panama base who had not seen an American girl for a year and followed

Cherry with his eyes, "because you kind of remind me of home."

They wanted Cherry to be mother and sister and friend, as well as nurse. She found that half her nursing was kindness. The boys were wonderfully cooperative, heartbreakingly grateful and uncomplaining . . . the most unselfish patients Cherry had ever had. Everyone of them was determined to get well quickly, so he could return to his soldier's work. "We can't win the war lying here," they said impatiently from their beds. "Besides, the Army's got a lot of new tanks and guns we haven't seen yet!"

As Cherry saw these men get well, and walk out sound and courageous, she was thankful that she was a nurse.

Her idealism grew, nourished by the everyday heroism of her soldiers. Her assurance grew, too, in her ability to succeed as an Army nurse. Cherry was trying hard to make a good record for herself. Perhaps some day she might win promotion to Chief Nurse—her youthful age was no handicap. It would be wonderful to be promoted! It would be proof to the world, and especially to herself, that her uncertainty about her ability to meet every test, no matter how severe, with flying colors was unfounded! Perhaps Cherry's assurance grew a little too heady as the month neared its close. Although she was not quite fully aware that she was in a mood for overreaching herself, a faint warning ticking in her mind reminded her that she was ripe for trouble. But it was very faint.

Cherry should have known better than to let Lex and Captain Endicott meet on her ward. She easily could have steered one young man one way, and the other young man in an opposite direction. She knew she should keep Bunce, particularly, away from that inflammable combination. She knew Johnny Mae Cowan was a stern Chief Nurse.

Lex and Paul came face to face late one afternoon on Cherry's ward. Rita was off duty, and Cherry and Bunce had been struggling all day, along with the other corpsmen, to get everything done. It had been an exasperating day. The medicines had not arrived, the hot water had been turned off, Williams's hot water bottle had cracked and flooded his bed, three boys had to have treatments every time Cherry turned around. Now, on top of it, Captain Upham and Captain Endicott were coldly facing each other across Williams's bed.

"You here again, Endicott?" Lex said caustically, as he looked over the charts Cherry handed him. "This seems to be your pet ward. Nurse! Why hasn't Lazlas been getting the bland diet I ordered?"

Cherry replied indignantly, "He has!"

Paul looked at her with a sympathetic grin, inviting Cherry to grin back disloyally over Lex's bent head.

She stiffened. "Do you mind very much, Dr. Upham," Paul said charmingly and dryly, "if Lieutenant Ames gives me my report now, or must I wait indefinitely?"

"You'll wait," said Lex.

"Certainly, Captain Upham," said Paul, with the faintest tone of ridicule.

Bunce, who was making the patients comfortable for the night, was working at the next bed. Cherry heard him say in a tired voice, "You're all set for the night, I guess. You don't need a back rub, do you?"

The young patient answered gamely, "Sure, I'm all right. I'm no sissy."

Cherry whirled and shook her head at Bunce. No matter how tired Bunce was, the patient's comfort came first. That boy had been lying there all day. Bunce should not ask the boy if he needed a back rub. He should roll him over and give him one. Lex too had heard. He glanced up with a warning nod at Bunce.

But before either Cherry or Lex could speak, Paul Endicott stepped over to Bunce at the adjoining bed.

"That's the kind of inefficiency my department wants to know about!" he said sharply. "Why do you let this boy shirk his job?"

Cherry rushed to Bunce's defense. Shirk, indeed! But Paul interrupted her.

"Bunce Smith's record is already open to question. Poor performance of duty like this should be reported!"

All Paul's charm was gone, as his gray eyes, on Bunce, turned cold and hateful.

Lex said quietly, "Smith is an excellent corpsman. Everyone slips up occasionally. You seem, Captain Endicott," Lex said bluntly, "to be maliciously looking for charges to pin on Smith."

For a moment, Cherry thought these two low-voiced men were going to strike each other. Their faces had gone white with hatred. She hastily started giving Paul his report, frantically maneuvered Lex to a patient at the end of the room, and signaled Bunce to get on fast with that back rub. Paul walked out with his report, still sneering.

Cherry felt exhausted by the suppressed strain of that clash. She went into the utility room and limply sat down. That was quite a revelation Paul had made! Charming as he was with Vivian, he certainly was petty and unfair with his subordinate, poor Bunce. Lex, bless him, had saved the boy.

Bunce stumbled in. He flopped down on a low stool at Cherry's feet. His youthful face was wretched.

"And I thought maybe if I worked hard, I could get to have dispensary training and be a technician, and earn a corporalcy some day!" he muttered. "Not a chance with that dressed-up taskmaster picking on me!"

"Never mind, Bunce," Cherry patted the boy's clumsy hand. "I'll recommend you and I'm sure Dr. Upham will, too." She did not mention what Captain Johnny Mae Cowan might do. The stern Chief Nurse probably would hear of this incident. Cherry dreaded that for Bunce's sake and also because Johnny Mae would mark "poor executive supervision" on Cherry's record.

Bunce dejectedly blinked his blue eyes. "And besides I'm *awful* homesick," he confessed. "Oh, gee, Miss Cherry, I hate this war. I want to win it, quick as we can, and go home."

"That's it. We'll win provided everybody works hard. And if you work, and if you keep out of trouble just a little longer, well, you'll be a technician yet."

For the few days left of November, Bunce was a model of deportment. It was so long since he had done any mischief that Cherry feared he was due to burst soon. She felt nearly ready to burst herself, after this crowded month of hard work. Thank goodness her day off was just around the corner. She would have her chance finally to go seeking pirates' rubies in the sand, and maybe even a ghost in that fantastic house.

"I may not find a thing, but," Cherry promised herself, "I certainly am going to have myself an exciting day off!"

CHAPTER VIII

A Ghost Returns

ON MONDAY, DECEMBER FIRST, THE ROSES WERE blooming, birds sang, and there was not a cloud in the sky —Panama City's nor Cherry's. She had been off duty since yesterday afternoon, and she was free until she started her new night duty at seven this evening. Cherry had spent the morning luxuriously asleep. After lunch, she had strolled down the famous promenade called Las Bovedas, which paralleled a crumbling granite wall along the sea.

Now, back in the main part of town, she passed the statue of Bolivar, the South American Lincoln. Under it lounged Bunce, dressed up in his best uniform, uncomfortable, hot, and grinning.

"I kind of figured you'd pass this way, Miss Cherry," he said as he fell into step beside her. "Gosh, you walk slow . . . little ol' chicken steps."

Cherry squinted up in the sun at her lanky, long-legged corpsman. "Bunce Smith, don't you know that an officer and an enlisted man aren't supposed to have dates? You mustn't be seen publicly with your boss."

Bunce grinned amiably and stubbornly followed her into the main shopping street. He was up to something, Cherry realized, and said so.

"Who, me?" Bunce said with an injured expression. "Why, I'm just goin' out to have a little fun. I might even do a good deed, or something brave, on my way. Uh . . . by the way," Bunce stumbled a little, "where're you going later? Going to that crazy house?"

"I won't tell you! Why do you want to know, anyhow?" Cherry asked suspiciously.

Bunce smiled broadly. "So you *are* going there! No fooling, Miss Cherry, maybe it isn't a safe place for you to go alone."

Cherry laughed. "Don't worry about Ames! Good-by till seven." She marched into a department store.

Cherry dawdled pleasantly over perfume and lace and fans, which her soldier patients had requested her to buy for them. She suspected some of the gifts were for her, for the boys had specified "something a girl like you would like." She paid for most of the things in United States currency, for some in silver balboas, and had her packages sent.

When she came out of the shops, the sun hung like a huge orange balloon over the low, flat, stone roofs. It had somehow got to be four o'clock. Cherry was very warm and thirsty. She found a sidewalk café, shaded by an awning and enclosed by pots of red geraniums. Gratefully she sat down and ordered a soda. It was a strange soda, lukewarm milk and syrup, and no ice cream at all. But if Cherry did not care much for her soda, there was someone who was staring at it with enormous, wistful brown eyes.

These fascinated eyes belonged to a nonchalant and jaunty urchin, aged about nine. Cherry stared at him; he stared at her soda. Only a pot of geraniums separated them; she took another sip, but those longing eyes would not let her drink. At last Cherry said:

"Would you like to have a soda, sonny?"

The little boy's brown face broke into a radiant and ecstatic smile. He made a hasty bow and slid into the chair beside her astonishingly fast. "Señorita, you are mos' kind an' you make me mos' happy an' I weesh you sousands of sanks. I'll like choc'lit."

Cherry was not surprised to hear this urchin speak English. Many citizens of Panama City, living next door to its American twin city of Ancon, spoke both Spanish and English as a matter of course. But as the waiter departed for the soda, Cherry observed with amusement, "That's a formal speech for a little boy."

The urchin blinked his great eyes at her and dangled his legs from the chair. "I am of E-spanish, and I am courteous." He was puzzled that Cherry should find his manner strange. He added politely, "The Señorita, she ees courteous also. She invite me to soda!" His eyes sparkled as the waiter set down a large glass in front of him. He pushed himself up on his chair, nestled his small head over the soda, and dreamily got to work on it. Cherry watched him, hugely entertained. Having noisily sucked up the last drops from the bottom of the glass, he wiped his mouth with a grimy little hand, and said:

"Now *I* do a favor. We are frands. W'at you like me to do?"

Cherry could not help laughing. The gallantry of this small tattered boy was out of all proportion to his size. "Thank you very much, you are most kind," she struggled to match his manners, "but there is nothing— Yes, wait a minute. You *can* do me a favor." She could do with some adventure after this month of hard work.

The little boy beamed. "Weeth great plasure."

"Take me to the deserted house on the lane."

The urchin's mouth dropped open. "Oh, no, Señorita! I would not take any señoritas to soch bad place."

"But if I ask you to?" Cherry persisted. "After all, we are friends."

"Frands, yes, and I do not weesh my frands go *there*." The child looked conscientiously at his empty soda glass, then back to Cherry. "Okay, I take you *almost* there."

Cherry followed the little boy along narrow side streets, and then into unpaved, hilly, even more tortuous streets. It would be almost impossible for an automobile to get through here. Cherry asked questions, but the child disapprovingly refused to talk. He led her to the lane which she remembered.

"Adios, Señorita. Thees ees bad reward for soch good soda." And then the child turned and ran for all he was worth.

She walked forward toward the house. It was a fantastic, ramshackle old house, overgrown with vines. Trees sighed against its faded walls. Mysterious houses fascinated Cherry. She picked her way through tangled weeds and flowers, passed a topless well, a sort of cistern, and came to broken steps. The door, unhinged, stood half open.

Cherry hesitated on the threshold. After the brilliant afternoon sun outdoors, she blinked in this musty darkness. Unable to see a thing, she stepped in. She stood there, listening. There was no sound except the creakings of an old house.

In a moment or two, her eyes became adjusted to the murky light. She was in a big square room, bare of furniture, its clay walls cracked and marked, its crude stone fireplace empty. Nothing to see in here, except some old crusts of bread and a pair of ragged shoes. She walked on to the next room. Here she found a broken chair and a great bundle of old rags heaped in the corner. Nothing here, either, apparently . . . then Cherry tensed. She distinctly heard footsteps beyond the doorway she had come through . . . not ten paces away from her!

They were slow, faint, unsteady steps. Cherry heard a long-drawn-out sigh, "Ay-y-y!" It was a man's thin voice. A shadow fell across the room where she stood.

Cherry's heart thumped in her throat. She could not take her eyes from that advancing shadow.

"Don't come any nearer!" Cherry thought frantically. "Oh, stay where you are . . . whoever you are!" She looked about desperately for an exit. But the only door was the one through which the shadow fell. She stared about looking for a window to crawl through. There was no window. She was trapped in an inside room!

The voice whispered again, like ghostly fingers brushed over harp strings, "Who dares to enter the house of the dead?"

With lowered eyes, she watched the dreadful shadow move closer. She could not raise her eyes to face whatever might loom in the doorway. The figure stretched out commanding arms, distorted in shadow on the floor.

"Leave this house! Leave unless you too . . . ker . . . ker . . . *choo!*" There was a loud sneeze, followed by a twangy Middle West voice exclaiming, "Doggone it!"

Cherry darted to the door. There stood Bunce, flapping his arms.

"Bunce Smith, I ought to report you for playing such a joke on me!"

Bunce rocked with loud laughter. "Scared, weren't you? Sissy! I only wanted to get you out of this dirty, deserted old house."

"I'm no sissy! And I'm going to stay if I want to!" Cherry exploded. "Here I hope to have some fun exploring this place, and you . . . and you . . . *sneeze!*"

"You have to admit I'm a pretty good actor," Bunce boasted.

Just then, they both heard a low cry.

"Was that you again?" Cherry demanded disgustedly.

"It certainly wasn't me, ma'am!" Bunce's clear blue eyes were mystified.

"It seemed to come from right in this room," Cherry puzzled. She looked around the windowless room, empty except for the broken chair and the big heap of rags.

Then the rags stirred. Cherry and Bunce looked at each other anxiously. "A tramp, I guess," Bunce reassured her.

But it was not a tramp. At least, not the sort of tramp they had ever seen before. As they stood watching, the top layer of rags went hurtling off, and a queer little man tried to sit up. He was small, with coppery skin, a rather flat, blunt face, and two black pigtails. He moved his hands helplessly and sank back into the pile of rags.

"He's sick!" Cherry exclaimed.

She ran over to the man and looked into a pair of dull, beady black eyes, offset by broad cheekbones. Bunce was right behind her.

"He's an Indian," he muttered. He fingered a hand-loomed wool shawl of rainbow stripes which the man wore over his rusty black suit and purple shirt. Cherry studied the stolid, copper-colored face. She had seen Indians many times in Illinois when they came into Hilton on Saturdays to market, but they had been much taller and lighter-skinned than this little man. Suddenly it struck her, she was used to North American Indians, this man must be either a South or Central American Indian!

But his nationality did not concern Cherry now. What mattered was that he was a human being, sick and helpless. He was shivering, his teeth were chattering, his face was wan, and his fingers had gone colorless. These were the symptoms of tropical fever . . . first stage.

"What's the matter with him?" Bunce asked fearfully.

"Don't you remember," she whispered, "what you read in Herold about malaria?"

Bunce swallowed. "Sort of similar, but this is a lot more severe! What kind of tropical fever is this?"

All the dread possibilities raced through Cherry's mind . . . this could be malaria, or yellow fever, or one of the unknown, uncontrolled fevers! And then she thought of something even worse—malaria cases in the Army were isolated, kept under control, the source of infection was known and fought. But here was this fever-ridden man wandering about, without anybody's knowing that the fever was abroad and unleashed without control. One sick person was enough to start an epidemic.

Frantic questions raced through Cherry's mind. Where had he caught it? Where had he been? From the looks of his battered shoes and his pinched face, he had traveled a long way. How long had he been in this house? That swampy garden was full of mosquitoes; let many of them bite him, carry infected blood, and a swarm of disease-bearing mosquitoes could descend on the city like winged death. Cherry thought fearfully of that cistern; it would make a fine place for mosquitoes to lay their eggs.

Abruptly she got up and ran out of the house. Pushing aside the heavy undergrowth in the garden, she located the cistern, knelt, and looked down into the stagnant water. It was hard to see down there in the late daylight. Yes, there it was! A grayish film of larvae floated on the dirty-looking still water. Mosquitoes were breeding here! They might or might not be disease-carrying mosquitoes. She ran back into the house.

"It's a breeding hole, out there," she announced to Bunce. Bunce's face grew worried as he began to realize the terrible implications of the man's illness.

Cherry started to question the sick Indian. He listened to her questions, his coal black eyes watching her lips. The stolid expression on his face did not change. Apparently he understood no English.

She suddenly noticed the man wore a ring on one of his fingers. She bent closer, breathing a silent prayer that it might give her a clue as to who he was and where he came from. It was a heavy ring of beaten gold and silver on which was portrayed a sun atop a mountain, a palm tree, and an Indian in a canoe. She slipped the ring off his finger and held it up before the sick man's eyes.

"Listen!" she said desperately. She pointed to his ring. "Where? *Donde!* Doctor! *Americano!*"

The Indian said something low-voiced in a strange tongue. "Must be Indian dialect," Bunce muttered to Cherry, "doesn't sound like any Spanish I ever learned."

The Indian was fishing in his pocket. He produced a tattered snapshot and held it out to Cherry with trembling fingers. She and Bunce studied it. It showed a young man, an Indian, standing beside an American soldier, both smiling.

"His son?" Cherry guessed. "He's on his way to find him?" Bunce shrugged and spoke to the Indian in halting Spanish. But the man did not understand Spanish, either. He was having such a severe chill that he was losing consciousness. Cherry looked at him in horror.

"So this is our ghost," she said in a hushed voice to Bunce.

"Haunted house, huh?" Bunce muttered.

Cherry said, "Don't you see? People think it's haunted because they see or hear things going on in here. This house is used as a way station, as a place to sleep, by wandering Indians! Didn't you see the food and the marks on the walls when you came in? It's Indians, not ghosts!"

"This is worse than any ghost," exclaimed Bunce worriedly, "this is death on the loose. Gosh! I do hope they'll know what it is and have the right treatment for it!"

"The right treatment," echoed Cherry. Dr. Joe and his new serum flashed into her mind.

Cherry was suddenly galvanized into action.

"Listen, Bunce! I have a plan. We've got to get him to the hospital, on the double. You stay here with him. Do your best to keep mosquitoes away from him. I'll come back with an ambulance."

Bunce gulped and agreed. Cherry snatched up her purse and hat, raced out of the house and sprinted down the lane. She remembered the way back to Ancon's main throughfare. There she caught the Army hospital bus, and in twelve minutes time she was back in the hospital lobby. She rushed to the telephone operator's room.

"Can you locate Dr. Upham for me?" Cherry asked her urgently.

The obliging operator tried all the wards. She tried the Operating Rooms, Major Fortune's laboratory, a research room, Lex's office. It was useless.

Cherry went back into the hall. At the end of the corridor, she saw a familiar little figure in nurse's uniform approaching her.

"Hello, Cherry. What are you looking so upset about?" Rita asked.

"There isn't time to explain now," Cherry said as she started to hurry on.

Rita's dark little face puckered up into a frown as she peered at Cherry's smudged face and soiled seer-sucker dress. "You'd better get yourself cleaned up for the ward. We're due to start our night duty at seven, remember, and that's less than two hours off. And Vivian says Johnny Mae is in no mood to trifle with."

"Thanks, Rita, but I'm in a big hurry now," she flung over her shoulder as she rushed out of the main building. She knew now what she would have to do. She had no authority to act on her own. But which came first . . . this man's life, and possibly many other lives, or discipline? But discipline was needed in order to safeguard lives, Cherry reminded herself. On the other hand, what about medical ethics? What about the dictum, "The patient must be saved at any cost"? The more reasons and arguments Cherry thought of, the more mixed up she became. Meanwhile, her feet were carrying her on, and her will was driving her forward to do what she most deeply knew was right. And she had not a minute to lose!

Cherry crossed the hospital yard to another wing. The sun was dropping and, though it was still daylight, the air had lost its warmth. She entered the Receiving Department and sought out Ann.

"Ann, could you help me get an ambulance?"

"Have you a doctor's O.K.?"

"No." Cherry added, "It's urgent. Take my word for it."

Ann's calm dark blue eyes studied her. "Is the patient an American soldier?"

"No, but you know we often treat anybody at all who needs care. It's awfully important that this patient be admitted."

Ann looked down, thinking. "It's awfully strange. I don't—Urgent. Hm-m. Wait here. I'll see what can be done."

Cherry waited as Ann disappeared into a small office. She emerged soon, her face expressionless. She said to Cherry:

"I can't take the responsibility of ordering an ambulance. But I put in a good word for you with the clerk. You'll have to talk him into it yourself. And oh, golly, how I hope you know what you're letting yourself in for!"

"I know," Cherry said grimly. "I also know I'm doing something necessary." She marched in to talk to the clerk. She argued, pleaded, coaxed, explained. How she managed it, she did not know . . . probably by confusing the clerk so much he did not know exactly what to think . . . but Cherry succeeded.

"We're short of ambulances," the clerk told her, "we can't send you one for half an hour."

In that case, she had better not wait to drive over with the ambulance. She would go ahead and relieve Bunce, so that he at least, could get to the ward well before seven. Accordingly, she gave detailed directions to the clerk for the driver.

Walking shakily out of the clerk's office, Cherry did not know whether she was glad or sorry that she had undertaken such an unauthorized responsibility. The minutes were spinning by faster and faster. She *had* to relieve Bunce quickly!

Cherry rode part way on the bus, ran the rest. She still had a chance of being on time herself if the ambulance arrived when promised. She fled up the lane.

The house, as she entered it, looked darker and more sinister than ever, now that twilight approached. She went through the door.

Bunce was still faithfully at the Indian's side. He looked up in relief when Cherry squatted down beside him.

"He's worse, I think," the boy said worriedly. "He's awfully hot, but his skin is dry as paper." In the half-dark, the Indian's face was flushed, his eyes were closed.

Second stage, clicked Cherry's mind, recalling what she had read. This was some form of malaria, all right!

"Bunce," she said in a strained voice, "you aren't going to like what I'm going to say, but well, it's an order. I want you to get back to the hospital and go on duty. You've done your part, and more than your part."

"And leave you alone in this deserted house?" Bunce shook his shaggy head. "I should say not!"

Cherry was firm. "It's an order. Please go. I have my reasons, Bunce."

"You'll come back with the ambulance?" Bunce asked anxiously as he stood up.

Cherry nodded. Bunce reluctantly left. She heard his footsteps in the next room, then on the steps. Presently they faded in the lane.

It was very dark and still in this inside room. The trees outside in the cool evening wind swayed and moaned. Cherry tried to settle the suffering man a little more comfortably on the pile of rags. She fanned him with her hat. "I hope," she thought somberly, "that Dr. Joe's new serum will cure this case." *Serum!* The sentence she had read reappeared sharply before her eyes——

"Severe rare form of malaria called blackwater fever must be treated with serum."

Cherry had a hunch that this was it . . . blackwater fever. Oh, if only that ambulance would hurry, hurry, hurry! A faint buzzing edged into her thoughts. Mosquitoes! Clearly, and distinctly she remembered reading these frightening words: "The fever mosquito, which spreads blackwater fever and yellow fever, is a night feeder and does not attack until sunset. It prefers light to dark races, and young people."

Cherry shivered. If these winged hypodermics had bitten the sick Indian and become infected . . . if a fever-bearing mosquito bit her . . . The whining buzz sang in her ears. She flapped her hat about steadily. She was tired and frightened. Her duty was to her patient. Stay here she would, at all costs!

The room grew darker and darker, and still the ambulance did not come. She would never get to the ward on time. Cherry hardly could see the Indian's face now. The buzzing grew louder, higher. She lost track of time, and in her fatigue and tension, still flapping her hat, relapsed into a sort of waking dream.

Noises outside roused her. She heard the throbbing of an engine, axles straining, and men's shouts. The ambulance! At last! Cherry ran through the two dark rooms to the door.

"In here!" she called. "Bring lights and a stretcher!"

She saw in the fading light, two men jump down from the ambulance . . . one was a most welcome familiar figure . . . it was Lex! Oh, bless him! Ann must have told him about her request for an ambulance. She ran down the lane sobbing with relief, "Oh, Lex, oh, Lex, I'm so glad *you're* here!"

The ambulance driver apologetically said, "We had a hard time getting this big car through the side streets. Hope your patient hasn't suffered by the delay."

Cherry smiled at him and said, "As long as you made it!" Then turning to Lex she rapidly explained the situation.

"And, Lex, it looks worse than malaria. I have a hunch it's blackwater fever!"

Lex let out a low whistle and said, "Come on, Cherry, let's have a look!" They went into the house and Lex bent over the sick man to examine him. When he straightened up, his face was very grave.

"Cherry, we've got a serious case on our hands. We'll have to act fast. We've got to report this case to Colonel Wylie for orders."

At the mention of Dr. Wylie's name, Cherry's face fell. "Oh, no, please, Lex, no! We can't. Oh, Lex, this is Dr. Joe's chance to use his new serum. Don't you see that Colonel Wylie will send this case to the civilian hospital . . . and poor Dr. Joe will lose this wonderful opportunity to prove his new serum? Lex, please," she pleaded, "can't we take him back to the hospital and get Dr. Joe busy right away? Lex, do you remember our dictum: 'The patient must be saved at any cost'?"

Lex yielded. "All right, Cherry, you win! We'll think about charges for breaking the rules later."

The strain was beginning to tell on Cherry. She felt sick. In a kind of miserable daze, she answered questions and filled out the ambulance report. At last they were off!

Back at the hospital, Cherry and Lex moved the patient into bed quickly . . . safely in quarantine. So far, so good. Then Cherry ran to the telephone and called

Dr. Joe. Relief sounded in her voice when she heard Dr. Joe's gentle hello coming over the wires. "Dr. Joe, this is Cherry. Listen carefully. I haven't time to explain now, so don't ask questions. Come right over to the hospital and bring your new malaria serum. We've discovered a case that may be blackwater fever. Yes, yes, we've got it right here in the hospital. I found the patient in a deserted house. No, no, we haven't reported to Colonel Wylie. We're doing this on our own. Please hurry. Lex will meet you in the lobby."

As she turned from the phone, she saw Bunce Smith loping toward her with open relief written all over his face.

"Miss Cherry, did the ambulance come? Is everything okay? Did you get the case to the hospital? I shouldn't have left you there in that house alone."

Cherry started to reassure him when a cold voice broke in. It was Captain Endicott. He had heard everything. Cherry groaned.

Captain Endicott's face was cold and forbidding as his eyes swept disdainfully over Cherry's disheveled appearance.

"I see. Lieutenant Ames and Private Bunce Smith are at it again. Lieutenant Ames, what is this all about? . . . a case of blackwater fever here in the hospital, brought from a deserted house . . . haven't reported it to Colonel Wylie . . . we're doing this on our own.

In case you are not aware of it, Lieutenant Ames, black-water fever is a job for the U.S. Public Health Service." His eyes glittered with hatred. "I suppose they, too, weren't informed. I shall report to Colonel Wylie at once." Sarcastically he added, "That's Army regulations, *Lieutenant* Ames!"

He wheeled about and strode purposefully off.

Cherry looked at her watch. "The time," she groaned. "I should have been on duty an hour ago." She hurried upstairs to Medical Ward, trembling at what she had done. It felt like a year, instead of a day, since she had hurried down these quiet, familiar, hospital corridors. She burst into the door of the ward to find Johnny Mae Cowan waiting for her. Rita, busy at the beds, looked up with a scared face.

"Lieutenant Ames, you are outrageously late!" the Chief Nurse declared. "You have been absent from the ward for an hour. Absence warrants dishonorable discharge!" She scowled at Cherry's soiled dress and rumpled hair.

Cherry was ready to burst into tears. "But I can explain," she pleaded.

"This is the Army! We want performance, not excuses! An order is an order!" Cherry knew it would be insubordination to argue with the Chief Nurse. An Army *no* was final. And she already had too many charges against her.

She was busy at her duties when the Chief Nurse called her and told her ominously:

"Colonel Wylie wants you to report to his office at once."

Cherry dragged herself downstairs really shaking with fear. This lateness—or the Chief Nurse might count it as an absence—alone could ruin her chances of promotion. "Promotion, indeed!" Cherry thought dejectedly. "When Colonel Wylie disciplines me as I deserve, I'll be lucky if I'm not thrown out of the Army Nurse Corps!" She numbly entered Colonel Wylie's office to face the anger and punishment she had brought down on her own head.

Captain Endicott and Major Fortune were both there, Dr. Joe and Colonel Wylie were in excited conversation. She blinked at them in the glare of the hanging light fixture. Colonel Wylie was coldly furious, threateningly still, as he looked up at Cherry. What could she possibly say to him? She *had* violated Army regulations.

"Lieutenant Ames," Colonel Wylie bit out, "what is this blackwater fever situation? Have the goodness to explain in full detail."

Cherry's throat was dry and tight. She told Colonel Wylie exactly what had happened, and that all her thoughts had been for saving the sick man and giving

Dr. Joe a chance to prove his new serum. "Please forgive me, Dr. Wylie, but . . ." Cherry stood there, her eyes stinging with tears. She simply could not bring herself to look at either Colonel Wylie or Major Fortune.

Colonel Wylie's expression had not changed during Cherry's recital. After a moment of dreadful silence, Colonel Wylie started to talk: "Lieutenant Ames, you have broken Army regulations. You realize the seriousness of that charge." Just then Colonel Wylie's technician-secretary entered the room to report the arrival of the men from the U.S. Public Health Service. Dr. Wylie had lost no time in reporting the case, Cherry thought.

Colonel Wylie asked to have them ushered in immediately. He gave the agents a rapid outline of the circumstances, then turning to Cherry he said, "This is Lieutenant Ames. She discovered the case. Perhaps you wish to question Lieutenant Ames?"

The agents asked the specific location of the house. Cherry told them and also reported the condition of the cistern.

The senior agent addressing Colonel Wylie said, "You know what this means, Colonel. We've got to inspect the house at once, get a full report on the immigrant Indian's true condition, and if there is any doubt about what particular fever or variant he has contracted, the water supply will be turned off and all outgoing ships will have to be inspected. Glad you reported this at once. Now, sir, may we see the patient for examination and our report?"

Colonel Wylie summoned his secretary, who, upon being informed by Cherry where the patient was quarantined, led them off.

Captain Endicott stepped forward. His face was pale with rage, further angered because his carefully laid plans for loaded ships ready to sail would be upset. He burst out, "This isn't the only outrageous thing Lieutenant Ames has done! It's time that someone reported Lieutenant Ames. She is inefficient. When I was checking up on the wards the other day"—Cherry caught her breath—"Corpsman Smith failed to do his duty and both Ames and Upham failed in their supervisory duties either to correct or report him!"

Cherry looked back at him, horrified. Colonel Wylie sharply addressed Cherry, "Well, Lieutenant Ames, have you anything to say to this charge?"

"It is a distorted account of what actually happened," she replied faintly.

"Certainly it is true!" Paul Endicott stated. "Lieutenant Ames is inefficient. I've witnessed her inefficiency. She——"

Major Fortune interrupted softly, "I think you have said enough for the moment, Captain Endicott." Paul deferred to the older man with ill grace. Dr. Joe looked unhappily at Cherry.

"There is no question that you did wrong, Cherry. But I appreciate that you were trying to do the right thing, even trying to help me where my new serum is involved. I know you've done this for me as much as for the soldiers. And I appreciate your loyalty," he encouraged her. She looked at her old friend with gratitude. "But Army discipline comes first. It must. And if it means that my serum isn't going to get a chance, well, that's part of the Army picture. You did break discipline, but it was with the best and most humane of motives."

Paul Endicott broke in angrily, "You should also know, Colonel Wylie, that Private Bunce Smith is just as responsible and involved in this as Lieutenant Ames. He is just as unfit——"

Colonel Wylie said suddenly, "That will do, Captain Endicott! Good evening, sir!"

Paul hesitated. Then he sullenly turned and stalked out of Colonel Wylie's office.

Colonel Wylie turned toward Cherry. His hawk face, his steely eyes, were as stern as Justice itself as he pronounced judgment on her in a cold voice. "You were trying to do the right thing, Lieutenant Ames, your motives were admirable. But you broke the rules. That cannot be tolerated. You are in the Army and we are at war. You must be disciplined."

There was silence. Cherry was thoroughly crushed by this time. Dr. Joe was such a pathetic figure as he looked at her with his warm gentle eyes full of sympathy that Cherry straightened up a little with the comforting thought: "I did do wrong, but at least Dr. Joe has a chance now to use his serum. Dr. Wylie has been so stubborn about it . . . he'd have sent the Indian to the civilian hospital . . . he'd never have brought the Indian here, where Dr. Joe can have his chance to prove his serum!"

She stood up a little straighter, bravely waiting for Colonel Wylie to name her punishment.

The surgeon was studying her, considering her case. His long pause made her nervous. Dr. Joe's face was anxious, too. Finally Colonel Wylie said:

"From now on, Lieutenant Ames, you, and Corpsman Smith, also, are on probation. You no longer enjoy full standing in the Army Nurse Corps. If you wish to remain in the Corps, you will have to prove yourself."

Cherry listened, too numb and stricken to move. Colonel Wylie opened the door. "You may go back to your ward now, Lieutenant Ames."

Cherry crept out, no longer caring what happened to her.

CHAPTER IX

Emergency!

THE LOW-SHADED NIGHT LIGHT CAST ITS GLOW ALONG the sleeping ward. It was a week since Cherry had been demoted to probation, but no new facts about the Indian had been uncovered. She tried not to think, as she wretchedly folded gauze sponges, of what a spot Captain Endicott had put her in. Lex knew of her trouble, but he was unable to help her.

A patient stirred and called. Cherry tiptoed over to him. He complained of pain, accepted a sedative gratefully. Cherry flashed her light on other beds as she returned to the night nurse's desk. Rita was on watch somewhere down at the other end of this spread-out ward. Bunce and the other corpsmen were working in the utility room.

Half past one. A flashlight blinked in the darkened doorway. Johnny Mae Cowan walked in. She sized up the ward first, then spoke to Cherry.

"Everything all right, Lieutenant Ames? Keeping your eye on Lazlas?"

"Yes, Captain Cowan."

The Chief Nurse lowered her voice. "You haven't been an Army nurse long enough to see an emergency, have you? War means casualties. Prepare yourself to face that fact. And be sure that everything is ready . . . complete in every detail . . . in case."

Cherry said in a somewhat shaken voice, "Everything is ready, ma'am. I hope . . . I hope we won't have to use our emergency preparations."

The Chief Nurse smiled grimly and looked at the empty beds with brooding eyes. Then she pulled herself up a little straighter, and said crisply, "Be prepared, Lieutenant Ames, practically and psychologically."

But as Rita reminded Cherry on the following long, tiresome nights, "There may be no emergency for us. Men wounded in battle are sent to hospitals nearer the battle areas. We can only wait."

Wait, wait! How hard it was for restless Cherry to wait! She was impatient to be sent to an active front. While they waited, the nurses prepared. In the afternoons, they had regular drill and a refresher course in some of the maneuvers Cherry had learned at Herold. Also, without warning, the nurses were now being taught field surgery. Cherry could guess only too well what that meant. One of these days her unit would be going right up to the edge of the battle areas, where surgeons operated instantly in tents on the most badly wounded. The nurses would have to know how to help the surgeons under these difficult, hazardous conditions. The girls wondered among themselves to what far and strange land they would go, and when. But there was no hint. On other afternoons, the Spencer nurses visited the Panama hospital of San Tomás, and invited the staff there to visit them in return. For as nurses, they were eager to become part of the community in which they worked.

Rita Martinez was very proud of Panama City's hospital. It was a low white palace building, set amid gardens facing the blue Pacific. She told Cherry about it on the long nights on ward duty. "You know we in Central and South America haven't nearly enough nurses or nursing services, like clinics, for good health," Rita said. Cherry nodded. "When you look at me," Rita continued, laughing and sticking her little nose in the air, "you are looking at a pioneer! Hospital San Tomás has one of the few nursing schools in Latin America. When I won my R.N., there were only twenty-one girls being graduated. They came from Panama and Colombia and Ecuador and Nicaragua and Peru and Chile, and all over. So you see our girls down here are beginning to study nursing and to do something about neglected health. Thank goodness our hospital gives scholarships. Like your Cadet Nurse Corps."

Cherry grinned at the pretty little pioneer. "Good for you!" she said. She thought about the Yankee nurses who went south of the border to teach and to help set up nursing schools. That was something Cherry would like to do some day.

Rita Martinez was a darling, Cherry thought, as Rita talked gaily to her these long nights. She realized that Rita talked partly in order to distract Cherry from her troubles. For Cherry was worrying.

On her half day off, Lex unexpectedly came for Cherry at Nurses' Quarters. She had not seen him since she had met him, for five minutes, to tell him of that terrible scene in Colonel Wylie's office. She was extremely glad and relieved now to have him turn up.

"Hello, you rock of strength," she greeted him, as they started off down the street together. "Where are we going?"

"To my office, where we can talk!" They arrived and shut the door. Cherry was anxious to know how the U.S. Public Health Service was making out with the case. Was it blackwater fever? Had they found out where the man came from and how and where he had traveled? And did they find the source of infection yet?

"This is how things stand," and young Dr. Upham told her the facts, which she as a nurse did not have access to. No one had been able to diagnose the Indian's disease, except that it was some obscure form of malaria. Therefore no one knew just how to treat it. Dr. Joe's new serum had been tried, but since malaria requires at least one to two months' treatment, it was too soon to know if Dr. Joe's was the right serum. The Indian, though very sick, fortunately held his own. "Probably," Lex said, "because he has lived most of his life outdoors and has a naturally strong constitution."

He added after musing a moment, "If we could only find out where this man has been! Then we'd have a good chance to learn what the disease really is, and how to treat it. He's still too ill to question, even if we could find someone who speaks his dialect. It's too bad," he continued, "an examination of his clothes before they were burned didn't reveal a single clue to his identity. Not a thing. There wasn't even a ring, which is strange because they go in for jewelry in this part of the world."

Cherry suddenly grabbed Lex's arm, and stared at him, wide-eyed with shock.

"What on earth is wrong with you, Cherry?" he demanded.

She did not answer him, but was frantically digging around among the contents of her purse and came up with a ring and a dog-eared snapshot, which she held before Lex. She swallowed hard, her heart was racing and her hand was trembling as dumbly she held both articles up for Lex to see.

"What are these and where did you get them?" Lex fairly shouted at her. Cherry explained how she had been studying them that day in the house and how in all the ensuing excitement she had stuffed them into her purse and had forgotten completely about them.

"Of all the silly girls—" He ran his hand through his stubborn light hair.

"Don't you call me names!" Cherry's already red cheeks flamed.

"I'm fond enough of you to call you names!" Lex shouted.

Cherry burst out laughing. In a moment, Lex was laughing too. "Just like old times," Cherry gasped.

But they both sobered very quickly when they realized how much precious time had been lost and that it might even make things worse for Cherry and Bunce—and even Lex who was involved with the two.

Lex studied the snapshot for a moment. "Mm!" he said, "a young Indian with an American soldier. It may mean that he's stationed at the Panama jungle base."

"Oh, Lex, that's a thought!" cried Cherry. "Do you think he is the old man's son?"

"He may be," replied Lex thoughtfully.

"What will we do, Lex?" Cherry cried in despair.

"That, young lady, will require some planning." Lex had to leave then, but promised Cherry he would let her know as soon as he mapped out a plan.

Cherry only wished she knew how to find the missing answers to the important questions and so help lighten the black cloud hanging over their heads.

Her own half day off rolled around again. Cherry was worried as she and Vivian, who had the same afternoon off, were upstairs in Nurses' Quarters, talking soberly about Cherry's difficulties. Ever since Vivian had learned how Paul Endicott had behaved, she had been appalled. This afternoon Cherry and Vivian were going over and over the stubborn facts for the dozenth time, hoping for an answer, when the phone rang.

It was for Vivian. From the troubled way she said hello, Cherry knew it was Paul Endicott, calling her on the house phone in the lobby downstairs. Cherry picked up her hat and purse, preparing to leave. She did not want to overhear, and she did not want to see that hurt look come into Vivian's sensitive face. She knew Vivian's allegiance was painfully torn between Paul and herself these days.

"No, no really," Vivian was saying to Paul on the phone. "I'm sorry, I can't see you today. I . . . I'm busy all day."

Cherry went out and down the stairs feeling embarrassed. Vivian was perfectly free to see Paul. Vivian was turning Paul down out of her loyalty to Cherry.

As Cherry came down the stairs into the lobby, Paul was just hanging up the receiver. Defeat and fury left an ugly, even nasty, look on his face. Cherry started to turn back until he had left. But his cold eyes held her on the bottom step.

"So you're the reason why Vivian is busy!" he said bitterly. That was all Endicott said before he turned away, but there was no mistaking the recriminatory note in Paul's voice.

For days, she thought about it with apprehension. Vivian was so unhappy that it made Cherry even more mournful. Cherry's additional worry about the Indian, even though good, capable Lex was working on it, made her a very miserable girl.

Suddenly all these worries, and everything else, were wiped out in a night of terror. About the middle of December, Cherry was on ward duty when she became aware of suppressed excitement and activity down in the moonlit hospital yard. She ran to the ward window. Every ambulance the Army hospital owned and several ordinary cars were speeding in, parking, racing out again, down a street which led to the docks. In the dark below, Cherry made out corpsmen carefully lifting litter after litter out of the ambulances. Long still forms under blankets filled those litters. Her ward phone was ringing like mad. Cherry dashed to answer it.

"We are getting three hundred new cases!" the Chief Nurse's voice said. Behind her voice, Cherry heard other excited voices, hurrying footsteps. "It's one of those freak things nobody thought could happen! American troops were just leaving Panama when an enemy submarine torpedoed a transport. Just off the coast! There was a terrible explosion . . . the ship limped back to port . . . there will be more casualties . . . these are only the first . . . what? Yes! Hold on, Lieutenant Ames!" Johnny Mae Cowan's voice receded, talking to someone else, then returned to the phone. "Now listen carefully! The injured already have had emergency first-aid care. You and Lieutenant Martinez are getting ninety-six of them." Ninety-six additional men to care for instantly! Cherry's hand tightened around the receiver. "Are you listening?"

"Yes, ma'am. Everything is ready."

"Good! Give the men a hot meal right away. The kitchens will be working all night. If they are too badly hurt to eat or drink, give them intravenous infusions. You'll have to manage it without a doctor, all the doctors will be operating. You'll have a lot of shock cases. Have the corpsmen get warm blankets and hot water bottles ready, and get ready to give blood transfusions. Understand? I'll be up as soon as I can." The Chief Nurse hung up.

Cherry got hold of Rita, summoned her nine corpsmen, and rapidly told them the news. They had to turn on the lights in the ward, and some of the boys in the beds woke up and realized what was happening. About a dozen of the boys who were convalescing struggled out of bed and into their bathrobes.

"We're going to help!" they said. "Besides, you haven't got enough beds up here. You give them our beds. We'll sleep on the floor."

"You can't!" Cherry said. "You're sick yourselves!"

"We know what it means to be wounded," they told her. "We'll help . . . you'll need us!"

The litter cases started pouring in. The stretcher-bearers and the corpsmen and the volunteering patients eased the suffering young men into the beds. Cherry and Rita worked over the worst patients as fast as they could. Cherry prayed that the plasma supply would hold out. Hot food had come up from the kitchen, but there was no one to serve it. What Cherry would not have given for a few student nurses to help! There was no one to prepare special shock beds either. Cherry dropped her own work for a few minutes to get the corpsmen started on that. Bunce understood, he quickly organized the corpsmen. Cherry sent the shaky but determined old patients to serve food trays under Bunce's direction. Meanwhile, the litters kept coming. Rita was still struggling with the worst of the shock cases. Cherry thought desperately, "Someone ought to treat and rebandage those wounds!" She herself raced to the severest cases with the dressing cart. Oh, Lord, there weren't nearly enough of them to help these men! No orderlies, no nurses' aides, worst of all, no student nurses . . . she ran to the phone. She tried to reach the Chief Nurse by phone but got the floor supervisor instead.

"I've got to have help!"

She dropped the phone and stared appalled at the crowded huge three rooms. Beds were pushed close together, every bed was full, and now they were bringing in sitting cases. There were no more beds! Boys among the fifty old patients who should not have been on their feet were weakly pushing themselves out of their beds, giving them up to their more seriously wounded comrades. And then those beds were quickly filled, and still more wounded poured in! They were getting the overflow from Surgical! Someone would have to get extra cots from the basement and set them up.

Johnny Mae Cowan sent up Red Cross workers, the unit's physiotherapist, the dietitian, and clerical workers. She promised that Panamanian Girl Scouts would come tomorrow. Everyone pitched in with a will. Cherry and

Rita set them to finding more beds, blankets, hot water bottles, making up medical records, wheeling out the patients' clothes, running errands. Cherry herself ran from bed to bed, picking out the most desperate cases. She remembered to smile and talk to each exhausted man, as her flying fingers examined and treated pain-racked bodies. The soldiers looked up at her with heavy eyes, and seemed to relax when she patted their shoulders.

The men were heroic. Cherry lost all track of time as she labored over one case after another. Not one of them complained, every one of them said, "I'm not so badly off . . . take care of my buddy first."

Somewhere around daybreak, Lex and Dr. "Ding" Jackson and Dr. Freeman came in. Their faces were haggard and unshaven, but they all worked with Cherry and Rita until the sun stood high in the sky. Cherry herself would admit no fatigue. A terrible urgency to keep going drove her on . . . especially as she saw once more how completely and urgently the doctor relies on the nurse. At one moment she found Rita leaning against the wall, her hands pressed to her temples.

"No, no," Rita brushed Cherry aside. "I'm not really tired. I'll be all right in a minute." And she went on.

Bunce was white with exhaustion, as he directed the other corpsmen and was in a dozen places at once. Efficient, levelheaded, almost tender with the wounded men, Bunce was wonderful this terrible night. Cherry took time to think, "He deserves a promotion, not probation!" The day nurses, Vivian and Bertha, came on at seven A.M. Johnny Mae Cowan came in to say that the night staff could go home or at least take a rest period and have some food now. But not one of them would leave the ward. For two hours more, they worked on through blinding fatigue. Suddenly exhaustion struck Cherry, and she crumpled up in the utility room.

Lex picked her up. "Go home," he said roughly, "and sleep." He half-led, half-carried Cherry downstairs, and put her on the hospital bus that ran to Nurses' Quarters. "Keep an eye on this girl," he said to the driver, and went back to his work.

Cherry voluntarily hurried back to the hospital three hours before it was time for her to go on duty. Vivian and Bertha were still on the ward, half-desperate for lack of student nurses, but trying to keep cheerful to comfort the men. "Everything all right?" Cherry said to Vivian.

"Yes." Vivian picked up a bottle of plasma and some rubber tubing, then turned her face away. Tears stood in her eyes.

"Steady now," Cherry whispered, and pressed Vivian's hand. "Here, I'll help you."

"Thanks, pal," Vivian whispered back. "I . . . I can't . . . those poor boys!"

"Thank God we are nurses!" Cherry replied sturdily. "*Our* pity *means* something! Come on, let's get to work." And they translated their pity into practical help.

That night and even the less turbulent nights that followed tested Cherry's idealism and her worthiness to be an Army nurse to the utmost. For all the tragic things she saw, there was no horror . . . she only felt, more strongly than ever before, the glory, the beauty almost, of the service she could give. That heartened her. But something else worried, almost frightened, Cherry. As the war deepened, and there were more and greater battles, more and still more nurses were going to be needed . . . if thousands of men were to be healed and returned to battle . . . *if we were to win.* Cherry wished she could cry out to other girls, and her voice carry beyond this crowded pitiful room, far across the Caribbean and all over the United States, how desperately nurses were needed.

Everyone was struggling through extra emergency duty. She saw Rita come in, then Bunce.

"*Hóla, ¿qué tál?*" Rita sang out cheerfully, but her eyes were anxious.

Cherry shook her curly head. Bunce managed to grin in the teeth of everything.

"Anyhow, you sure reformed me," he said. "Between that crazy house and these last few nights, I guess I'll *stay* reformed this time."

"I reformed you," Cherry replied, "by getting you put on probation! It's I, not you, who needs reforming."

Things gradually began to calm down. At least there were no more new admissions. Cherry and Rita got things under control in the overcrowded ward and running with as much smoothness as so few of them could achieve. The Chief Nurse had not given Cherry one single word of approbation for all her efforts during the terrible emergency, although she had publicly praised Rita. A little encouragement would have meant a great deal to Cherry as, under the strain of probation and waiting and worry, her self-confidence sank to a dangerously low ebb. Of course, Lex always had a bracing word for her. Ann and Gwen and her other friends tried to reassure her. But they could not help her solve the mystery. Now Cherry had time to worry once more about the mystery of the Indian. Something had to be done and done soon. Too much time had elapsed as it was! She wanted desperately to get Bunce cleared and into Medical Technicians' School.

Bunce did not reform entirely, and it probably was to the benefit of the soldier patients that he did not. He came into the ward, in the third week in December, with a black eye. Grinning, he boasted how he had got it. There had been some sort of pre-Christmas fiesta, and Bunce had tactlessly won all the prizes, for marksmanship, foot racing, and boxing. As if this was not enough to enrage the local boys, all the girls had admiringly trooped after Bunce. The soldiers, weak on their pillows, were delighted with Bunce's black eye.

Almost Christmas! Cherry had not realized it. Almost her birthday, too, on the day before Christmas. The Indian had been lying in the hospital, sick and silent, for close to a month now. And still no one knew how to cure him, nor what the danger of an epidemic was.

One afternoon several of the girls were in Nurses' Quarters, wrapping up little Christmas gifts to put under the ward Christmas trees for their soldier patients. Bull sessions among the nurses were frequent. Today the girls sat cross-legged on their double-decker beds, before piles of candy and cigarettes and small books and red tissue paper, and discussed everything from hair styles to the latest medical discovery. Ann, as usual, was a little apart, her gifts were already wrapped and she was study-ing for the promotional exams. Cherry once had studied too. But in her despair, she had given it up as a doomed effort. The girls' chatter turned to the subject of boys.

"By the way, Cherry," redheaded Gwen said, licking a silver paper star, "your friend, Captain Endicott, has had an awful lot to say lately."

"What is he saying?" Cherry looked up startled from the package she was tying. "And to whom?"

"Oh, he's all over the place, making a great row, spreading unfriendly gossip about Bunce, and about you . . . and griping because of the fuss everyone is making over the Indian you found,"

"And that's not all!" Vivian stood in the doorway. They all looked up. She was panting, as if she had been running. "Paul Endicott is in Colonel Wylie's office right this minute, trying to make an appointment for next week to see the ANC officials to . . . to bring charges against you and Bunce and maybe Lex! He's angry about those ships of his . . . and he hates *you.* Cherry! He's charging inefficiency and . . . and . . . He's going to try to get you all dishonorably discharged!" Vivian fought back tears. "Oh, Cherry, Cherry! I never want to see Paul Endicott again!" She dropped onto her bed, pulling off her hat and crying.

Bringing charges! Against all three of them! Dishonorably discharged! Cherry jumped to her feet. What a spiteful, conniving, rotten way for Endicott to behave!

Suddenly Cherry jammed her hat over her black curls and snatched up her purse. She ran back to say to Vivian, "Oh, Vivian, don't take it so hard." But Vivian was crying uncontrollably. Cherry tried to soothe her. There was nothing she could say that helped. Ann came over, and motioned Cherry to leave.

Cherry ran out of Nurses' Quarters and headed for Lex's office. They had to solve the mystery of the Indian before Paul complicated things even more.

Fortunately Lex was in. "Ding" was in, too, but tact-fully manufactured an errand, leaving them alone to talk together.

"Do you know what Endicott is doing?" Cherry demanded of Lex. She told him what Vivian had reported. His eyes grew dark with anger and worry. Cherry ripped off her hat.

"Here, sit down, Cherry. I've got things to tell you. I looked up those decorations on his ring. Those are Mayan historical symbols on the ring. But they apply to almost any part of the Andes mountains, whose branches range through many Central and South American countries. So what we need is an interpreter. I took some people who speak South American dialects in to see him. After a lot of trouble, we got the Indian to say a few words. But the interpreters couldn't understand him. They thought he spoke Mayan, a separate language. Yesterday, I had some luck. I met a man here in town who keeps a bookshop. He's quite an expert on languages. He's coming here today to see if he can do the interpreting job and if not, he's promised to find us an interpreter."

"I see," exclaimed Cherry. "The interpreter will be able to tell us whether the young man in the snapshot is his son and whether he's stationed at the Army jungle base."

"Bright child!" teased Lex. "Then we can arrange for the son to come here. His son can tell us exactly where the old man came from and by what route. Then we could figure out the source of infection and make our report to the authorities."

Cherry nodded vigorously. "And the young man might even recognize the disease. He might have seen it before!"

"Right, Cherry. Let's keep our fingers crossed that our bookman does a swell interpreting job. Then we'll move *fast*."

"Oh, Lex," wailed Cherry, "we've got to before Endicott has a chance to make those charges!"

Lex put his arm around her shoulder. "And then, with luck, you and Bunce and I would be out of this mess. And I hope even Vivian will cheer up. Well, Cherry, the picture looks brighter now!"

Cherry said warmly, "Thanks, you old . . . old friend in need!"

Once Cherry and Lex got things moving, they did move fast. Lex phoned Cherry that night to tell her the great news. The Indian had talked a little. Yes, the young man in the snapshot was his son. He had heard that the boy was injured, and had made the long trek through the Andes Mountains to see his boy. And yes, the son was stationed, or had recently been stationed, at the Panama jungle base! Lex dispatched a letter instantly to the Army base, enclosing a copy of the snapshot and a sketch of the ring to identify the young Indian.

Cherry was in Lex's office the following day when he received a long-distance phone call. From Lex's end of the conversation, she gathered that the call came from the Commanding Officer of the jungle base. He had the young man there and he was granting him a leave for this emergency.

"Thank you, sir. We won't keep your man long," Lex promised.

The next day, a quiet young Indian arrived at the hospital. He was tall, slim, straight, with coppery skin and straight blue-black hair. He seemed almost American, with his tan sports suit and woven black and white shoes. He spoke English. He had been, since his teens, a ranch and plantation hand in Texas and some- times in Mexico. When the war broke out, he had volunteered his special Indian knowledge of the mountains and the jungle. They asked him his name. "Eef I tell, you cannot pronounce," he replied gravely. "Jos' call me Joe."

Joe, and Lex, Major Fortune, and Cherry all entered the older Indian's sickroom. The patient was asleep. Cherry gently roused him.

The little old man looked up and saw his son. His beady black eyes blinked.

Joe said something in the strange tongue. The old man closed his eyes in assent. There was no outward sign of affection. Joe talked, questioned, waited. The old man, with an effort, replied. The son nodded, looking satisfied. Cherry gave the old man a drink of water, and Lex gave him back the original snapshot and the ring. The Indian spoke to his son, handing him the ring. Then his own nurse came in, and the visitors left.

Once outside the door, Joe relaxed. But the others remained tense until he finished telling them the facts for which Cherry had been waiting so long.

The old Indian had started from his obscure home in the jungle. He had traveled by foot for six days. Four days before he reached Panama City, he had pushed through a wild, primitive lowlands, alongside a river. Lex was following what Joe said on a pocket map. "Then the source of infection would be about here!" Joe verified the location. Most important of all, the young man had seen this disease many times before, and recognized his father's illness as a specific form of blackwater fever.

Cherry was thrilled. The Indian would be cured now. Dr. Joe's serum and new Diesel oil sprays could be used with sure knowledge, instead of just experimentally . . . the U.S. Public Health Service could notify the Indian's native country of the place of infection . . . the danger of epidemic was averted . . . the problems were solved! And Cherry and Bunce were cleared!

Her spirits lifted for the first time in a long month. Cherry turned to Joe and said, "I don't know how to thank you for coming!"

The young man replied, "I thank you, mees, for I get to see my father. And *he* thank you—" he pressed the strange and beautiful ring into her hand "—for saving hees life."

Cherry accepted the ring with thanks and good-bys.

"I have to thank you too, Cherry," Major Fortune said. Such relief was in his seamed face! "I'm going to see Colonel Wylie immediately!"

Lex and Cherry were left alone.

"How are you feeling, Lieutenant Ames?" he inquired politely.

"I am feeling very, very much relieved!" she replied. "In fact, Captain, now that the truth is beginning to dawn on me, I am beginning to feel wonderful!"

"Hold on, Cherry my girl. We've got another very important part of our job to do and it may be very unpleasant. Were you forgetting that Lieutenant Ames and Captain Upham must report their findings to their Commanding Officer, Colonel Wylie, at once?" Lex tried desperately to lend his question a light touch, but he could not keep a note of apprehension from creeping into his voice. Seeing Cherry shrink, he tossed off lightly, "Here's a talisman for luck, Cherry. We'll both need it." He kissed her gently on her forehead. "Ready?" he asked. Cherry straightened up. "Ready!" she said. They hurried to Colonel Wylie's headquarters, anxious to get the unpleasant task over.

Colonel Wylie listened to Lex's report and refrained from making any comment during the entire report. When Lex had finished, Colonel Wylie immediately reached for a telephone and called up the Public Health Service to relay the important information on to them. These were the findings of Lieutenant Ames and Captain Upham of the U.S. Army Medical Corps, he said into the phone. There were several moments of silence in the room while Colonel Wylie listened to the voice at the other end of the wire. A very faint metallic sentence: "These two people are to be congratulated, Colonel Wylie," came drifting into the room. "Harumph!" exclaimed Colonel Wylie as he hung up.

Colonel Wylie fixed his steely gray eyes on both Cherry and Lex. "In addition to the other charges, you now have charged against you the suppression and withholding of important clues. You may leave now. You will hear further in due time."

Lex and Cherry, on exchanging notes after leaving Colonel Wylie's office, both agreed he had not sounded too gruff.

They walked back to Lex's office. Lex had something more to tell Cherry. When the door was closed behind them, Lex asked Cherry to let him look at the Indian's ring again. With a puzzled frown Cherry handed it to him.

"You know what that ring is? It's a birthday present," Lex reminded her.

"Gosh, today *is* my birthday! I'd entirely forgotten!"

"The day before Christmas," Lex confirmed, "I have a birthday present for you, too, if you'll accept it."

Lex's present was a ring, too. An engagement ring. An old-fashioned gold and opal ring which was a family heirloom.

Cherry gasped and admired it. Then she looked dazedly and affectionately at Lex. "You . . . you can't propose to me in a hospital office! And anyhow, even though Army nurses are permitted to marry, I don't know what to say! I don't even know," she wailed, "if I want to get married yet!"

Lex smiled gamely. "All right, Cherry, you think it over. I know you've been out of school only a few months, and I don't want to rush you. I . . . I suppose I ought to make a romantic speech about love, but I'm not very good at that kind of stuff. Anyway, you already know how I feel about you."

Cherry seized his hands and held them tight in her own. "Lex, you're the best fellow I ever knew, or ever hope to know," she said softly.

A bell rang in the corridor.

"Seven o'clock," she gasped. "I'm due on duty! Lex, forgive me for not answering now. Honestly I don't know what to say . . . and I've got to run!" But she stood there, hesitating, reluctant to leave him.

Lex strode to the door and smilingly held it open for her.

~~~~~~

CHAPTER X

Special Mission

LATER THAT EVENING, WHILE CHERRY WAS ON THE ward, the phone rang.

"Lieutenant Ames, report to Colonel Wylie's office immediately!"

Colonel Wylie faced Cherry across his desk. "Pack your things at once, Lieutenant Ames!" he ordered. "You are taking a plane in an hour!"

Cherry clung to the edge of his desk. She thought desperately, "They must be sending me home! They *are* discharging me from the Army Nurse Corps!" She glanced pleadingly at Bunce and Dr. Joe and Johnny Mae Cowan, who were standing in Colonel Wylie's office looking mystified. In a weak voice, she got out, "Where am I being sent, sir?"

205

"To the Pacific." Colonel Wylie chuckled at Cherry's look of amazement. "Major Fortune's serum has been used on the Indian for three weeks now and we finally see signs that it can cure blackwater fever. You are to deliver Major Fortune's priceless new serum to a Pacific island Army hospital. His colleagues there, who have been working unsuccessfully on the same thing, are waiting for it. These research doctors will develop the serum further, for there are actually cases of blackwater fever in the Pacific area. It is the first of the serum ever to be sent and you are the first Army nurse to be entrusted with a special mission of this kind." The surgeon added dryly, "It is a very great honor."

The faces of the other three in the room lighted up with excitement and pleasure.

Cherry thought she would faint. "I'm going to . . . fly? To the Pacific? To bring Dr. Joe's research friends his new serum?"

"Yes. Now you, sir." Colonel Wylie turned to Bunce, who paled. "Private Smith!"

Bunce shuffled his feet. He was past being able to talk. Cherry held her breath. She was safe, but what was going to happen to Bunce?

"I have here," Colonel Wylie barked, "recommendations for your admission to Medical Technicians' School and for your promotion to a corporalcy, from Lieutenant Ames, Captain Upham, and Chief Nurse Cowan."

Cherry glanced up at Johnny Mae Cowan, surprised and pleased. So she had put in a good word for Bunce! And for Cherry, too, apparently! The Chief Nurse smiled back at her a shade reprovingly.

Colonel Wylie cleared his throat. "I also have here . . . hmm . . . a very bad report on you, Smith, from Captain Endicott." Colonel Wylie silently read over Paul's charges. "Very bad indeed. So bad, Smith, that I think I shall disregard Captain Endicott's report entirely."

Bunce forgot himself and whooped. Everyone in the room laughed, and Cherry and Bunce were pumping hands in a joyous handshake. Colonel Wylie, still chuckling, rose from his desk to shake hands with Bunce.

"I'm happy to be able to give you this opportunity, Private Smith. You seem to have uncommon medical ability. I understand that you hope to become a doctor some day. I sincerely hope that attending Medical Technicians' School will be a step toward fulfilling your ambition."

Bunce blushed to his ears, and said, "Thank . . . thank you, sir!"

Colonel Wylie nodded his acknowledgment of Bunce's gratitude. "Smith, you pack too. You sail late tonight, back to the United States to attend the School." Bunce's blue eyes were dancing.

Colonel Wylie's secretary stepped in to announce that Captain Endicott had arrived.

"Oh, yes," Colonel Wylie said dryly. "Just ask Captain Endicott to wait."

Colonel Wylie turned to them again. "I wish to point out something more important than your personal fates. That is the medical victory which has been achieved through Cherry Ames's courage, alertness, and initiative. And through the unselfish assistance and dependability of Corpsman Bunce Smith. Major Fortune's successful discoveries will be announced to the medical world and to the press immediately, but naturally the formulae will remain a military secret. The United States Public Health Service will later standardize Major Fortune's new spray control, serum, and vaccine. Once more we can be sure that Panama is the healthiest spot in the tropics, thanks to the Health Service. One more thing, Lieutenant Ames. You will find a very pleasant surprise awaiting you at the Pacific base hospital."

"A combination birthday and Christmas present," Dr. Joe beamed proudly.

"What? Oh, what is it?" Cherry begged. She looked from one smiling doctor to the other. "Am I going to stay in the Pacific? Or am I coming back? What about Lex and my friends in the rest of the unit?"

"An important promotion and a new post await you," Colonel Wylie said, trying to sound gruff. "You'll see your friends again soon. Now run, young lady! A plane is waiting for you!"

Cherry shook hands all around and ran out. Dr. Joe and Bunce followed her. Going through the anteroom, they had a glimpse of a dejected Paul Endicott. They heard Dr. Wylie summon him, then the door closed.

Cherry, for all her haste and joy, looked back curiously. What was going to happen to Endicott? It was Bunce who blurted out, "Say, Major Fortune, what's Colonel Wylie going to do with that guy?"

Major Fortune hesitated. "I don't want to speak out of turn. But you'll hear about this, anyway. Colonel Wylie feels that Endicott has been malicious and meddlesome, and has acted outside of all bounds of his duty, and that he could be more useful working with a different sort of personnel. So Colonel Wylie is transferring Endicott."

"Transferred!" Cherry exclaimed. Colonel Wylie certainly had handled matters in his own inimitable way. She could not summon up any pity for Endicott. If she felt sorry for anyone, it was for Vivian whose eyes were open at last. But she was really thinking of Lex. She wished Lex could have been present . . . a large part of this triumph was his. And what a triumph!

"I've got to run!" she cried to Dr. Joe and Bunce. "There's a plane waiting for me . . . imagine!"

She dashed off down the hall, and the full realization of her triumph burst upon her. So she had not only regained her old status, she had won this honor *and* a promotion! She'd ask to take the promotional examination later, anyway, she'd want to. And Bunce was going to Medical Technicians School! Life was wonderful again!

What to do first? She'd have to tell Lex she couldn't answer him now! Jam a few things into her suitcase. She'd ask the girls to pack and send on her foot locker by boat. Say good-by to Ann and Gwen and Rita and Bunce. She wished she could cable her family. Her family . . . Midge . . . Charlie . . . Today was Charlie's birthday too! Cherry's throat tightened. Then she thought how proud Charlie, and her mother and father would be of her, and ran like mad to get things done. So she had thought she had failed, and how gorgeously she was vindicated! What a surprise! What a birthday! Flying away on Christmas Eve!

Cherry got to the airfield in a jeep, on time for once in her life. A great four-motored plane, nearly a block long, a bomber, waited. Her jeep driver told her that this bomber, stopping here for refueling, was on its way to rejoin a fighting force, also delivering supplies . . . "and delivering you too!" Under the bomber's great spreading gray wings, in the twilight, stood Rita and Bunce—Johnny Mae Cowan had let them leave the ward!—and Johnny Mae herself. And Ann and Gwen . . . how had they managed to come too? And a dozen of the other Spencer nurses and doctors, and several of her nearly well soldier patients, and, best of all, Dr. Joe, carrying a bundle, and Lex.

Cherry ran to Lex first of all. "You understand, don't you, Lex," she asked urgently, "that I can't decide now?"

"Of course, Cherry, of course! And I'm mighty proud of you!"

"It was your doing," she said gratefully. "If it hadn't been for you, Lex . . ."

"Nonsense, you did it yourself!"

All the others stood around watching and smiling, but Bunce edged himself in. "Gee, thanks for reforming me, Miss Cherry. It certainly was worth it, wasn't it? Now maybe I'll be a doctor some day, at that!"

"This," said Cherry with a grin, reaching in her purse, "is to wear, to remind you to *stay* reformed." She handed him the Indian's ring. Bunce drew in his breath, thrilled, but he did not want to take it from her. "No, I want you to have it," Cherry insisted. "It's too big for me, you see? And it will be good for your conscience." She hesitated. "Well, so long, doc. And good luck to you, Bunce!"

Bunce looked like a small boy about to cry. "I'll see you again some day, Miss Cherry, see if I don't! I'll write to you!"

To Ann and Gwen and the other girls, Cherry said good-by with the happy assurance that she would be seeing them all again before long. But saying good-by to little Rita Martinez was hard, for she probably would never see her again. Rita knew it, too.

"Good-by, Rita," Cherry said soberly. "You've been a good friend to me."

"*Adios, amiga. Vaya con Diós.* Go with God."

Cherry turned quickly to Johnny Mae Cowan.

"Thank you, Captain Cowan," she said simply.

The Chief Nurse shook Cherry's hand. "You're a fine nurse, Lieutenant Ames. Perhaps you yourself," she said wisely, "will be a Chief Nurse one of these days!"

Two men of the ground crew began to chase them away from under the wings as Cherry turned last of all to Major Fortune. "And what about you, Dr. Joe? Where will you be?" she asked anxiously.

"I don't know, my dear. But wherever I go, or wherever you go, we'll both know that it was you who brought my new serum to complete success." The pilot, the copilot, three gunners, the radioman, the navigator, young Army Air Forces men in clumsy flying suits, strode across the airfield. They clambered into the huge waiting plane. Cherry had only a minute or two longer. Dr. Joe hastily thrust his packages and some letters into her hands. "These letters just arrived for you from home. Take care of yourself, Cherry! And write!"

"I will, I will! Good-by, everybody!" Cherry cried as now the great propeller started and roared in a whirl of dust.

"Good-by, Cherry! Good luck!" her friends chorused over the tremendous noise of the bomber's four engines. "Happy landings!"

Johnny Mae quickly introduced Cherry to the pilot of the bomber, and he led her to a ladder on the side of the plane.

"Up you go!" said the pilot, over the din.

"Lex!" Cherry turned around halfway up the ladder to say one more good-by to Lex. Then the pilot pulled her through the small steel door, slammed the door, and Cherry bent her head as she climbed up the slanting plane floor. She sat down trembling on a narrow sort of bench. The engines roared, a flag dropped on the field, and the great plane trembled and shot forward. Cherry looked through the thick window to see Lex and Dr. Joe and Bunce and all of them rapidly growing smaller and dropping away as the plane lifted and soared and left the earth behind.

The plane flew high above the sea now, roaring out over the blue Pacific. Cherry looked back and down at the shimmering white spot that was Panama City. She had not found any pirates' treasure there, but she had found something vastly more important—a way to save lives!

So she had thought she was a failure! So the answer to whether Cherry Ames could stand up to the rigors of Army nursing was emphatically, yes! She had faced the grim tests and proved herself as an Army nurse at last! She felt more mature, more sure of herself, happier, than she ever had before.

Cherry settled herself on the seat for the long flight. She looked forward into a blue vastness of sea and heavens. The plane was heading for the jungles—perhaps for the smoky, deafening air of battle. Cherry did not know what new life she would find there, what new challenge she would face. But whatever it was, she was ready for it!